STRONG PAGANS
AND OT

STRONG PAGANS
AND OTHER STORIES

MARY O'DONNELL

POOLBEG

A Paperback Original
First published 1991 by
Poolbeg Press Ltd
Knocksedan House,
Swords, Co Dublin, Ireland

© Mary O'Donnell 1991

Poolbeg Press receives financial assistance from the Arts
Council/An Chomhairle Ealaíon, Ireland

ISBN 1 85371 123 3

Cover design by Chris Reid
Set by Richard Parfrey in Palatino 11/14
Printed by Guernsey Press Limited
Vale Guernsey Channel Islands

"Scavangers", "Widow", "Come In, I've Hanged Myself", "Halley's Comet" and "After the Match" were published in "New Irish Writing". (*Irish Press* and *Sunday Tribune*)

"The Estuary" and "Honey Island" were broadcast on RTE.

"Strong Pagans" won the William Allingham short story award in 1989.

"After the Match" won the Listowel Writers' Week short story competition in 1990.

Mary O'Donnell is the author of a collection of poetry, *Reading the Sunflowers in September* (Salmon Publishing, 1990).

For My Parents

Contents

Breath of the Living

There was a story she had once read about a cow which gave birth to a stillborn calf. The island farmer dragged the slimy creature across a field to the cliff edge and threw it down to the shore. But the cow followed the scent of her dead calf, nosed the wet birth-smell through the grasses until she came to the cliff. She sought a way down for hours. Finally, a giant wave swept in and over the body, increasing the beast's desperation so much that she jumped from the cliff in an attempt to claim her calf.

It was a story which settled more deeply in her mind as time passed, the kind of story at which some people might nod their heads, as if something were confirmed, something shared wordlessly, the intent of which extended even to the human race. She could recall lazily formulated mumblings about "instinct", "the power of nature" and "the call of blood".

Another story cohabited with this one. She read it by chance in an English newspaper, a report on a new messiah whose miracles were causing wide-spread hysteria in Kenya. One day, his female companion and helper incited a crowd to stone and batter another woman who was said to have slept with ten men and as a result became barren. She worried at this story for a long time, emerging dissatisfied with the inconclusiveness of the matter and her inability to forge peaceful terms of agreement.

Most of the year, the stories lay dormant, even companionably. She had little time to consider their implications. Occasionally as she rushed to class 5J or 3K, head bursting with the urgency of revising yet again the declension of German adjectives, she would remember—but fleetingly. Such things were of no consequence at all. She could laugh and dismiss them nonchalantly as the class rose and a chorus of "*Morgen, Frau Nelson*" filled the room. She knew that the forty minutes must be fully exploited, that the four or five brilliant ones must have enough to keep their minds ticking over, the mediocre pushed and encouraged, and the very dull made at least enthusiastic. Only the dull and the brilliant truly interested her. Near-remedial cases who at the end of a term could actually speak some German were the real victories, the ones for whom writing and spelling comprised a bleak and primitive tracking across a page—awkward of hand and mind—and yet in them there was something precious, kindling in her a need to seek it out.

That year, when tests had been corrected, reports written-up, the exam classes settled into state examinations, Elaine visited her parents for a week. She was in the happy and exhilarated state which marked the start of any summer: the weeks stacked endlessly ahead, her mind full of plans, the prospect of new gigs with the trio, new music to play and absorb. She felt pleased with herself and the year's work, as intact as she'd ever been. On the bus south she anticipated smoke-filled sessions at the casual jams in the city which she and two friends played every summer, hummed a new piece and considered the bass arrangement. Sunlight fell across her face while she rested her head and basked in warmth. Life had never been fuller.

The farm was large and extensive, with another hundred acres in tillage in the next county. A herd of Friesians were managed at the home place. David rarely accompanied her at that time of year, preferring to spend a few days on a cycling tour of some remote headland in the west or south-west. It was one of their blessings, she thought, as the bus lurched across the town square, the evening light making the familiar buildings seem like something golden and kindly from a nostalgic film. They were free as birds, took separate holidays not for the sake of escape but because it suited, because they could.

Her father was at the kitchen sink, hands slicked with Swarfega as he removed the day's grime.

"Hello Dad, how're things?" she called, dumping her travel bag on the floor.

"Dry," he muttered, smiling at her awkwardly.

"Don't whinge—it could be worse," she said.

"Ah, we could do with a spot of rain—the place over the way's parched."

"It'll come. Don't worry." She paused. "Where's Mum?"

"Out. Bridge I think, though it's hard to keep track of that woman's movements at the best of times," he grumbled amiably, drying his hands. He peered at her.

"Well, so how're the teachers?"

She grinned.

"Off for another three months, by God ye have it easy!"

So it went. Small-talk. Tentative openings. The rites of renewal of a contact which each time seemed more remote. Later, he took his seat in the sitting-room with her, lit his pipe and placed one foot against the mantelpiece.

"How's David keeping?"

"Oh. Fine. In good form."

"Good. Good." He was silent, watched spirals of smoke above his head.

"He went down to Slea Head yesterday with the bike." She switched on the television.

"Is that so? Good idea. Exercise."

They both stared at the last minutes of a soap which ended with a shooting and loud music.

"I like David," he said.

"Well I should hope so after ten years!" she laughed. He looked at her then.

"Yes. I like him. He's had his disappointments."

She said nothing.

"So have you, of course," he added matter-of-factly.

She switched channels restively.

That night she gazed at the ceiling of her bedroom and listened to sounds beyond the open window. The familiar droning from the creamery skim-milk plant, cars roaring down the road until well after three, late-night couples heading back from local hotel discos to their villages and farms further north in the boglands of Offaly. She remembered the dream she had had the month before when she had awakened with a shout. David had groped for her hand, sleepily, uselessly. In the dream, she had stared into the eyes of a woman. In them on some fierce night a beast rampaged across the dark dilated pupils, maddened, nostrils moist and running, its flanks steaming. The madness had clearly infected the woman, for she too was berserk. The howl from her throat was what woke Elaine, an awful howl which seemed to reach her ears from the centre of Africa, and her only recourse was to shout back, to answer with an open throat. She had lain a while afterwards trying to be still. But the birds beneath the eaves were noisy and she twisted restlessly in spite of herself. It would soon be that time of year, she had thought, when the gentle prodding and prying would begin. As soon as she got holidays, more than likely. That year, she had resolved to deflect all queries resolutely.

Now she thought again about the cow. Its impulse had something to do with nature outraged by injustice, pounding with the easy passion which was called instinct, the reckless search for union. She sighed in the dark. The things one imposed on other creatures, the concepts with which one juggled! The bloody cow went daft after the calf and jumped off the cliff. No more and no less. Her thoughts wandered then to the stoned Kenyan woman. She imagined her in the dusty heat, dressed in a black djellaba, head and hair covered. That was, if she were a Muslim. Then she conjured her again, this time with black skin exposed, the tight hair plaited and beaded. Elaine had often longed to take a piece between her fingers, just to see how far those tight kinks could extend. The stoned woman. She imagined tallness, long bones, strong teeth and sloping brown eyes. The tears she must have shed. In private. Years before the stoning.

She shuddered in the bed, her eyes on the moon's fan of light as it spread across the room through a slit in the curtains.

The house was usually noisy in the mornings. Doors with half-broken locks and loose handles were slammed to ensure closing. Funny the things they didn't bother about. Bloody right too! She heard her mother go downstairs; then came the sound of the water system, kicking-up as usual, an uneasy symphony of excess pressure which caused the pipes to groan.

"Sleep well?" her mother asked, moving lightly around the kitchen.

"Best kip I've had in ages," said Elaine.

"You can take it easy now you've got holidays."

"Yeah. I've plenty to do though." She filled the kettle with water.

"Did I mention we've got a new gig starting next week?"

"Oh? When did this come about."

"Recently. It was always on the cards. I told you before, remember? Our annual thing—me and Jean and Cora."

"I'd forgotten I suppose. Juice?" said her mother, proffering a jugful of orange juice.

Elaine nodded, held out her glass.

"Good as a hotel this," she said, after swallowing a mouthful.

The prelude could always be anticipated. There would be chance remarks about a cousin marrying, or somebody's daughter having another child after a series of miscarriages. She had to hand it to her mother, for sheer brazen neck. The established procedure was that Elaine would remain non-committal but politely interested for as long as the marriage and birth listings endured. Once or twice she might attempt to divert conversation from its well-trodden path by referring to one of the highlights of the school year or by chancing some amusing classroom anecdote. It was a gentle effort to avow her existence, to claim a life.

Useless of course. By the time the second cup of tea had been poured and her father had gone to supervise the scalding and disinfecting of the milk-churns, it began.

"Well," her mother smiled over her raised teacup.

"Here we are," said Elaine, smiling back.

"So. How are things?"

"Things? Great. Couldn't be better. I can hardly wait to start playing again. We've at least three gigs lined up now—it's a nice way of spending the summer," she rattled enthusiastically, buttering a slice of toast.

Her mother took another sip of tea as if considering, looked out the window, then back at her daughter.

"Now don't bite my head off, but could I ask...I mean..."

Here it came. She regarded her mother, wide-eyed, enquiring.

"I was just wondering if you've thought any more about that other matter?"

The Kenyan woman stirred from the ground where she lay; struggled to her feet.

"What other matter?" Play dumb. She thought of

the woman's hennaed fingers, blood-smeared now, saw her brush the smaller stones and chips of gravel from her clothes.

"Adoption."

"Oh."

Now a cow careered along a cliff-edge, its hide ruddy and white, plastered with rain.

"No. Haven't given it any thought."

Forward and back it went, hooves sinking perilously close to the edge, eyes rolling, the smell of still flesh rising on the wind from the shoreline.

"You could be denying yourselves a wonderful opportunity."

Her mother sighed and shook her head.

"You might regret it in years to come," she said.

"Oh for God's sake!" her patience was shredding. "Regret what? What have you ever done apart from rear me, how can you have any idea of fulfilment, without ever having done something else as well?"

It was a challenge. It wasn't what she wanted to say. These were the strict polemics of defence. She would try again. The Kenyan woman's face was bloodied, her hair glistening and matted. She would be gentle, reasonable.

"I want you to try very hard to understand this," she began, heard her school-teacher's tone, filled with the patience she used with potentially disruptive pupils as a method of disarming them.

"Dave and I are quite happy in our lives. Isn't that wonderful, Mum?"

She nodded her head to emphasise the words. Her mother said nothing.

"We lead very full lives. And I've been working

all year. I'd like a break now, OK?" she repeated.

She reached across and pressed her mother's hand. That morning she had space within, room to extend herself, to be reasonable where it was patently not required. She congratulated herself on her own generosity.

"How do you know you'll always be happy, that Dave will...?"

It came like an unaimed salvo which unexpectedly devastates.

She left the kitchen before her anger surfaced as it had done the previous year. She went up to the bathroom and kicked the door shut with all the viciousness she could muster. "Bitch, bitch," she whispered over and over into a hand-towel. It smelt clean and comforting. Good God were they never satisfied? They were the only people in the world who would dare turn the firm earth to a quagmire. She went to her room to dress. It still felt like hers, all those years on, and she thirty-three. She remembered a poem in which the poet fretted about the approach of middle-age, his own fallibility: "...for they are not made whole that reach the age of Christ." She had reached it herself now, the age of some sort of Christ, whoever or whatever he was. And we all know what happened him with his bright ideas. They crucified the poor bugger, a man who never married, who travelled with tramps and vagrants half the time, one woman at least crazy with love for him, and he as fertile as anything. If he had sons they never said. Or daughters for that matter. Battered a beautiful mind and body, tore it to pulp, split the bones in his hands with nails and let him asphyxiate on a cross.

She stayed for a week nevertheless. Her father was glad of help in the byre. Morning and evening she stuck the clusters over the teats of forty-five beasts, sat and listened to the rhythmic chugging of the milker, with sweet odours of hay and cud and cow-shit all about, content enough to be up to her eyes in the casual earth, away from the sanitary milieu of work. But her mind rambled. Forward to the gig, her fingers working through new chord sequences. She could use the octave technique, then dispense with the plectrum altogether after the forty-bar sequence. And backwards, perhaps for the last time.

It was a final evocation of the demented cow that jumped, blood-stormed, drawn by the smell of a dead calf. Herself and Dave. As if they hadn't done enough, been through enough. Their travail was so utterly private, a thing at which outsiders could merely claw with degrees of curiosity which varied from the harmless to the malicious. As if they hadn't gone half-mad with grief for what they never had and never would have. Sitting on a bench in the byre she grimaced at the air. She began to pray for the Kenyan woman, an informal benison. That she would have peace in her days. She prayed for herself. She was thirty-three. She massaged the palms of her hands, saw punishment meted, heard peasant and tribal phrases and the word which cut to the bone. Barren.

On her last evening, she prayed more than ever, to herself and to the spirit that guided her. For relief of pain in the face of pity. Their pity, which was for Dave. The bones in her palms seemed to split beneath a force driven with a too-human venom. It was deliberate. Her own father and mother joined the stoners, the blamers. Bones cracked in the evening light. There came a hoisting, a cool sense of elevation by brute strength. At thirty-three, she would not be silent. A figure staggered from the open dust towards the shade of a fig-tree. Their voices joined over thousands of miles. It was a high keening, a steady howl for a planet and its miseries.

The Deathday Party

S ecretly he'd hoped he might make it to old age. But no. The previous week it was confirmed. No. 3427189, white Caucasian male; residence Melmont, Ireland; name Dermot Baxter; Despatch date 03 May.

"The bastards," he grumbled to Grace, "couldn't even wait until after the holiday." Grace had booked Thailand only the previous month, a cultural tour which was to include a thorough induction in the more esoteric aspects of Bangkok's underworld. He'd heard that all the tastes could be accommodated, even Grace's. In the years since official coupledom, he'd never been able to satisfy some of her tendencies, had grown weary of bathing her wrists where the coarse sisal ropes cut and of tending other abrasion marks on her flesh. Sometimes he believed she took advantage of his being a doctor.

"Gracie!" he called. "Breakfast!"

He knew she'd be slow to rise. He poured himself a mug of coffee, sat down and thought lightly. This was it. What all the celebrations were about. Melmont was a place of outward jubilation. He couldn't pass a hotel or a pub, couldn't drive through the rows of dockland homes, without noticing festivities of some sort *en route* to his house-calls. Sooner or later they called your number. Nobody missed the Evening Deathlines on TV. There were usually sixty or seventy, depending on how many births there had been the previous week. What was important was the maintenance of balance. Eugenics. He stretched across the table, opened an ornate lacquered box and carefully chose a reefer.

It was a brilliant day, sharp with light and blossoms. He rose and opened the patio doors, momentarily cursing the swine that had ordained his death on that particular day. Still. No point moping. You only live once and all that. All in all, they'd had it good, he and Grace.

Standing on the patio, mug of coffee in one hand, reefer in the other, he considered. It had taken time to adjust to the notion of Despatch, Deathlines and Deathday. He'd been a child when it started: remembered the strikes and lockouts that took place during the first year and how the Chinese had overcome the blockade in the major European cities by flying in and dropping supplies—daily— throughout those months.

In spite of strikes and frozen economies, people were still hungry. They ate. Soon some of the advantages of Changeover became evident. The cycle of famines in the southern hemisphere ended. In the north the concept of guilt vanished, and churches were renovated as pleasure palaces. There were always the few who hadn't changed, for whom Deathday meant the beginning of another life, who prepared for it according to the old ways. Dermot

18

smirked as he thought about them. All in all he'd adapted pretty well. He watched a thrush rooting in the shrubbery to the left of the patio. The prospect of Deathday had defined his quality of life. It had been fun. Varied.

"My head...my bloody head..."

It was Grace. They'd been at the Deathday celebrations of an old friend the previous night. Dermot felt a bit queasy himself. They stood naked on the patio. Houses were warm, and the New Sensuousness had affected everybody. If it felt good, you did it. The day was warm. Despite occasional reservations about Deathday and Deathlines, Dermot conformed. His mouth curled downwards in disapproval as he regarded Grace's wrists and ankles. He couldn't remember exactly what had happened the previous night.

"Who was it?" he asked gently, through a smoke-haze. It really was too much. The woman would have her body destroyed. Some spectacle that'd make on her own Deathday. "It was delectable. Dee-lec-table!. Frankie did it for me..."

She poured herself a coffee, reached for the bottle of Ecstasy then paused as if deciding whether or not to take one.

"No. Better not. Later."

Dermot nodded in agreement.

"Take it at the do."

"He's so obliging, that boy!" she went on, a trifle unnecessarily, Dermot thought. "May be. But mind those ankles Gracie or they'll swell. Can't have you looking like—well, you want to look your best tonight..."

He was reluctant to criticise. She ignored him anyway. He became aware of her glancing at him from time to time, hoped she wasn't thinking too much. It was—despite his own inclinations—not to be encouraged. He recalled with satisfaction the night the philosophers were offered their options. Early Despatch, or community working cleaning up after the Deathday parties for the rest of their lives. Oddly enough, quite a number had opted for the former. But little pockets remained, had formed an underground Ecstasy resistance group. It was well known, half-tolerated. Beatrice, his own sister, was one of them. Just so long as they didn't get grandiose notions of their function in the scheme of things. Moreover, he was fed up treating torture cases, usually philosophers who'd been brought before the authorities and reminded of their decision to opt for community work. Once again, they were offered early Despatch but this time it was reinforced by a few twists of the thumbscrew, a day or two on the rack, or even, as in the case of two well-known recalcitrants, a week in the "violin" as it was called—a wooden double-ended violin-shaped head-trap. Indulging in private thoughts was one thing—everybody did it in private—that was acknowledged—but bonding together with like-minded thinkers was a subversive activity.

Dermot and Grace decided to have another go after breakfast, another swing before the party, when anything could happen. He mounted her on the bed. Later, she mounted him. He had to admit to feeling something, a twisting within. Nostalgia in advance of Despatch, he reasoned. All very natural. After all their time together, after what seemed like legions of other partners, the holidays, Deathday parties, state gang-bangs in mid-winter and Ecstasy Week in spring—Grace was, he believed, the only one who meant anything. Sloppy old Grace with her slightly sagging skin, heavy stomach and raw wrists and ankles. She was kind, always had been. There was something else too, but he couldn't think too much about that. The forbidden four-letter word beginning with L and ending with E. Once you got into that area you began to think. Really think. It was a boom time for psychiatrists.

"Darling, what should I wear?"

Dermot always consulted Grace on his attire.

"The pink suit or the turquoise?"

He posed with both before the mirror opposite the bed. Dammit but he was good-looking. He sighed, had hoped for many more Deathdays which were not his own. Such fun, such bloody good fun. Pity it had to come to an end. Life was so colourful.

"Go for the turquoise," Grace advised after a quick but penetrating look.

"It suits your skin tone," she added.

She opened her own wardrobe. Things hadn't changed so greatly for women since Changeover— at least, in matters of clothing. Cleavages were probably more appropriate than ever, but fatness was now respected: it reflected fullness of living. It was a point of pride with Grace to display her belly at such parties and, two years before, she'd had a diamond-encircled ruby implanted in her navel. Dermot approved. It suited her. There was little chance of her being mistaken for one of the PWs.

They were penned-in at the breeding unit beyond the city, away from partners and family, the obvious sources of stress. Any woman found smoking during her time faced immediate Despatch after the foetus had been removed for experimentation. Population stability was everything. Germany, which was top-heavy with elderly people who should have been Despatched years ago, was often pointed to as an example. Of course, the Germans got things confused. Something to do with war memories, Dermot thought.

"Wear your white-sequined two-piece," he urged.

"You think I should?"

In spite of himself, Dermot's heart leaped. Grace could be so vulnerable: she seemed at times to forget that her own decision was what counted, especially in important matters such as dress. But then again, he was no different.

"I think you should," he replied, kissing her again.

"It's going to be...different," she laughed pulling away.

"After?"

She nodded.

By five they were ready. Grace had rushed around, checked arrangements at the Hotel Tranquillia, hounded the florists until they produced the blue South African orchids she'd ordered, checked and re-checked with the caterers. At five fifteen they were driven by Despatch courier to the hotel, escorted up the red-carpeted steps and brought straight to the Ecstasy room on the fourth floor.

Lights blazed and an arc-light swung down. They smiled and waved. Dermot was widely known. He had always conveyed the impression of being an exemplary non-thinker. The clapping and stamping continued. His eyes scanned the crowd. They were all there—about four hundred well-wishers—friends old and new. He even noticed Beatrice doing her miserable, sisterly and philosophical best to smile and cheer. He assumed she was still in the Ecstasy resistance group, battalion C. Such notions, he thought. He gazed—gratified—at a haze of extravagant feathers, flowers, jewellery, brocades and silks. The air was spicy with perfumed skin. "We want Dermot!" the guests began to chant, slowly, but the sound gathered in volume, a tidal force which swept them to a pitch of enthusiasm that Dermot could only have dreamt of. He was flattered.

"We want Dermot! We want Dermot! We want Dermot!"

The jubilant cheering stopped as the room darkened and Dermot and Grace were ushered to elevated thrones at the centre of the crowd. It was time for the film. He glanced at Grace. She seemed happy. He wasn't quite sure how he felt. He hadn't taken his Ecstasy, postponed it until the meal. They settled themselves as "Dermot Baxter, No. 3427189— A Life" rolled up on the big screen. Grace squeezed his hand excitedly. People always enjoyed a good film. It was a tribute and a reminder. All the highpoints, the achievements and a few of the disappointments, provided they were disappointments over which a person had triumphed.

He watched now, fascinated. Childhood. Funny how he never knew he was being observed. Where the hell did they hide those cameras? His first date. A disaster. He regarded the spotty face of his one-time companion with distaste. She'd been a lousy kisser. Early Despatch for her, to his relief. The years at college. He'd been a wild one all right. Lots of booze-ups and gang-bangs, even then. He wondered how he ever got through his exams. "Dermot, you old ram," he thought satisfiedly. Then Grace. He was momentarily startled. She'd been slim then and unlined. So had he of course. Looking around in the semi-darkness he realised that they were all what would have been called "obese" in the old text-books before Changeover. No kids either. They hadn't been chosen as breeders, partly because of Grace's superior skills as a linguist. Something of a polyglot, she'd been instrumental in facilitating the smooth-running of the annual Changeover proceedings, spoke the Indo-European languages, and possessed a competent grasp of Swahili and a couple of the other African tongues. Africa had been difficult, he recalled. He focused on the screen again, recalled the moments of significance and the little moments: Dermot and Grace eating breakfast, summer 1970; Dermot and Grace in the bath, winter 1974; Dermot and Grace in bed, 1976, judging by the length of his hair; Dermot and Grace in fancy-dress during Ecstasy Week. They both laughed outright at this, remembered how they'd recaptured the effect of old-style clothes before Changeover. It had gone down really well—he in a pin-stripe suit, carrying a briefcase, Grace in a prim striped dress with a ruffled neckline, her hair specially greyed for the occasion. That had been a good laugh. Everyone had said they were models of successful modern coupledom.

The film faded gently to the closing bars of a

modern concerto. People applauded again, rose enthusiastically from their seats and turned towards Dermot. Despite himself, he was moved. It meant something. He automatically censored himself. "Meaning" was an *out* word, one which, as much as possible, you avoided mentioning. Made life much simpler, more enjoyable. The buffet tables were piled high with food.

"Really enjoyed that, Dermot," somebody murmured to him.

"Thanks," he replied, recognising a partner with whom he'd had a brief homosexual fling.

"Congratulations Dermot—a great life!" somebody else said, elbowing past him to the bowl of sugared almonds and cream sauce. It was Frankie. People had headed for the buffet tables almost immediately. No doubt he'd contact Grace afterwards.

"A life of achievement and fun," a woman said in passing. He couldn't remember her name but knew they'd coupled some time in the past year. He wanted to stay near Grace. It was not obligatory for him to circulate and collect another partner that night. She hovered nearby too. He poured himself a gin and drew from his jacket a packet of Ecstasy.

"Want one?"

"Give me two," Grace said.

"Sure," he said.

She popped them hastily into her red mouth.

The music was deafening. Out of the corner of his eye he realised Beatrice was moving towards him. Damn her. He hoped there'd be no nonsense. The rest of his family had been Despatched years ago. It was beyond his comprehension that Bea had been kept so long. He braced himself.

"Bea darling!" he gushed, embracing her energetically.

"Don't 'Bea darling' me!" she snapped, smiling back at him. She was cold as a stone, her pupils totally undilated. She wasn't taking her Ecstasy, he concluded, mildly horrified.

"Behave yourself for God's sake!" he said between his teeth, smiling broadly.

"It's not too late, Dermot, you could still leave with me—you could join us!" she whispered urgently.

"Don't be ridiculous..." he snarled in a staccato voice.

"You've never outgrown the old ways, Dermot. You're still a believer, a thinker, a searcher like me.

She gripped his hand in desperation. Her eyes welled up and to his dismay he saw that she was on the verge of tears. Mourning. Grief. That kind of thing.

"Not now Bea," he hissed warningly, then raised his voice again. "Isn't it a magnificent turnout—I'm amazed, quite amazed..."

"You could still join the Group!" she whispered again. Tears flowed in earnest now. Dermot broke out in a sweat.

"D'you still suffer from hay-fever? I could treat you very quickly—you should have come to me sooner," he said conversationally.

"Dermot..." she blubbered, "...you're my only remaining family...I don't want you to go...I *love* you!" she all but shouted then, clinging to his sleeve.

He tried to shake her off. Grace glared across as if to reprimand him for being unable to control his sister. There followed a brief, rigid silence as the word hung in the air. Most people pretended not to have heard the obscenity.

"What are you saying?" he almost shrieked. "How can you be so coarse at my Deathday party—so damned inconsiderate!"

That did it. Two women approached them.

"Is she bothering you?" one of them asked. He nodded, smiling. Again, for the second time that day, he felt a slight twist of something disagreeable as they took Beatrice firmly by the elbows and began to lead her away. She was still crying.

"Don't let them take me! I love you!"

The commotion could still be heard from outside the Ecstasy room.

"What a disagreeable scene," Grace sympathised to a man who was flirting with her.

"Quite," the man replied, looking closely at Dermot, who instantly recognised another possible successor to his wife's favours.

He felt a strange sense of disappointment. The pills hadn't worked properly. By now he should have been fully integrated, affectionate, joyful. Instead he was merely quite happy, the spectacle of his sister being led away to certain Despatch annoying him in the same way a small fly does when it keeps settling on your face. But by nine o'clock, people were ecstatic. Clustered in small and large groupings, they lay on the floor, stroked and touched, gazed into one another's faces. Dermot and Grace were also entwined affectionately. It was permissible. Not long now, he thought.

"Have you any more?" she asked, searching his

pockets for the white pills.

"No," he replied a little despondently. "We've used our quota for the week."

"Oh."

"Sorry about that. You'll be without until Sunday..." He sounded apologetic.

He knew what would happen. They both did. He'd opted for a saline intravenous shot preceded by Ecstasy. It was quick and painless. You went immediately. The heart simply stopped. Some people preferred a dose of barbiturates, freely chose a long, slow sleep into death. Dermot had never been one for delay, thought briefly and uncomfortably about Beatrice again, decided then that it was best not to think at this point, on the final stretch between life and death. There was no knowing how they'd despatch her. Fleetingly, he recalled a childhood incident, not on film, her fall from a tree when he'd pushed her in a fit of mischief. She'd wept then too. Again came the twist which did not signal a heart-attack but a pain which he dared not analyse.

"I'll be off in a few minutes," he remarked to Grace.

"Yes," she said, lying limply in his arms.

"Thanks...for everything."

"It was good," she smiled.

He knew by the way she stroked his face over and over that she was saying something else, a wordless thing.

The doors to the Ecstasy room opened. Four Despatch couriers dressed in official uniform arrived, their epaulettes gold-braided to mark the occasion of another joyous Despatch—the successful conclusion of another Deathday party. Dermot rose. To his surprise, nobody seemed to notice. A sense of recognition filled Grace's eyes but vaguely. It wasn't as easy as he used to think.

Widow

The coffin disappeared quietly behind the curtains in the crematorium at Glasnevin. She had seen to everything, from organising the service to comforting stunned relatives when she herself stood tearless. There were no feelings with which to grapple. It was an unmediated cerebral acceptance. Afterwards, they crowded around, pressing her shoulders occasionally, clasping her hands intently, and she sensed their compassion, aware that their pain would be indignant and short-lived. "So young..." someone behind her sighed. "It's always the same..." the voice went on, "In the prime of life, he had so much to achieve..." before petering out to an asthmatic sob.

Back at the house she breathed easily, relieved that it was over. The women moved around her, passing plates piled high with salads, and dessert-bowls which wobbled with pavlovas and cheesecakes. You could always depend on the women in time of bereavement. Lisa spoke to all her comforters, said what she knew they would wish to hear. Indifferent to their presence, whether they came or went, she spoke the words which would soothe them in their sympathetic anguish.

"Don't know how I'll manage," she shrugged her shoulders helplessly at Marian. "I can't believe it. I really can't take it in…" The friend shifted comfortingly.

"Of course you can't," touching her arm familiarly. "But you know we're all with you in this. You know that, don't you?" Lisa nodded. "And anytime, anytime…" Marian gripped her arm even harder this time, "that you need to talk…you know what I mean…just shout." Lisa looked at her.

"Thanks," she replied in as grateful a tone as she could muster.

The place smelt like a party. People laughed, then suddenly checked themselves. It had been a massive haemorrhage which struck on the way home from the city, right in the centre of his chest. He had managed to drive the rest of the journey, arrived gasping and white. Later that evening, he had died in the hospital theatre.

Booze and cigar-smoke wraithed the air. She sat back on the old leather sofa which still bore the green and blue woven blanket they'd bought one year in Morocco, and inhaled the atmosphere. It could have been one of their openings or even the small exhibition they'd held in the studio the previous spring, when small hordes of art lovers had trooped across the cracked yellow tiling that led to the annex behind their house. The art lovers could never decide how to behave, she thought a little amusedly. Whether to appear silent and awe-struck, as if they were on the site of a temple of worship of an ancient deity, or whether loud nonchalance was best. The terracotta exhibition, as she'd referred to it since then, had been a mix of refined and sometimes awkward silences and elegant outbursts of laughter, depending on who was there. Much like the funeral, she thought. The aorta had ruptured. She played with the word *aorta*, tongued it around her mouth. The simplicity of the words had astonished her with their weight of intent, the television soap-opera line "I'm sorry Mrs Jordan—we could do nothing..."

She observed an artist friend on the other side of the room as his lips rounded on a fork full of food. For a moment, her thoughts blurred, lost their razor-sharp coldness. Was it a party after all? Mental focus hardened once more, and the discomforting sense of fracture left. They were celebrating death after all, mollifying what they did not fully understand, by eating, drinking and laughing, in the hope that they could frighten it away. That the spectre would not come too soon. It was the dance of death, a courting of favours. By celebrating, while believing they were mourning one of their number, they were in fact preening themselves that they had survived and that they could escort death to the very peripheries of their lives.

Marian stayed for a week. Lisa did not sleep any night, which came as no surprise. It was part of the rite. She was alone. She would grow accustomed to aloneness. Initially she decided that the best way to accentuate that aloneness and get the painful aspects sorted out was to leave Alan's bits and pieces exactly as they lay. The steel edge of grief had to be faced head-on. People were kind, and not just for the sake of it, but sensitive too, perceptive of her needs.

Spring had come early that year, and with it an

inner exasperation at such gentle winds, such frenetic blossoming everywhere. The world spilt its kindness on her with a cruelty she had never before experienced. Her calmness and the routine quietness with which she coped disturbed the family. Yet there seemed no point in tearing her hair before them. Life could always be reduced to coping situations. Still, there were times of admission when she longed to race to the top of Killiney Hill and beat her chest while she screamed out at the sea. There were certainly times when the coast road and the broken paths which led to the shore might provide a sinister invitation.

Gradually, she disassembled Alan's belongings. He had masses of underwear which she had discovered when rummaging through the back of the airing-cupboard one day. She had thrust her face into a pile of his vests, disappointed when they didn't smell of him. Just washing-powder, fresh laundry, warmth. His jackets had hung for months before she even looked at them. They too had their odour: a tweedy mixture of tobacco and oils from the ancient brown one he used to wear in the studio; more delicate aromas from the other two. After-shave. The smell of a man. That was when she began to clench her fists and stand silently for minutes. The smell of a man. It was, she knew, the real beginning of her term. Lonely as opposed to alone. A place like Alcatraz. This was the start and there might be no escape.

She had entered the studio one day after work. The gnawing and yearning had begun in earnest. It was as if she were in solitary confinement, as if she could observe herself doing time with grief, could map her own progress day by day.

After much fiddling with the key, the rusted lock yielded. Inside, everything lay beneath an indistinct swathe of white sheets. She wondered if Marian had covered the canvasses during the week she stayed. She began to remove the sheets, sneezed as she did so, then opened the cracked yellow shutters that kept the room in shadow. Sunlight streamed promisingly into the place and she stood for a moment idly transfixed by minor maelstroms of dust that spiralled everywhere. The canvasses lay stacked against the walls, finished and unfinished. All oils. He'd finished with acrylics the previous year, she remembered. "No subtlety," he'd commented at the time, "all cut and corner—which is grand if you're a draughtsman." She'd recalled how he'd stood back appraisingly from the piece on which he was then working, his remark hanging non-committally on the air between them. "Oils," he'd said then half-teasingly, cleaning his brushes, "are like women. They flow into everything, mould their characteristics to any mood, defy rigidity of thought..." He'd stood there absently, watching the canvas before him, as if he were addressing it rather than her.

The last piece lay unfinished, just as he'd left it the day he had died.

It was the head and shoulders of a young man. The model had come to the funeral, was extravagantly and noticeably distraught. She recalled the face, twisted in an expression of near-despair. There it was again, she thought, but quite different. Alan had caught the seed of humour in the boy, had gained access to the secrets of his imagination. The young face before her was unsmiling; yet laughter lay not far behind the skin of his contoured face. It was the eyes that registered, forcing her to smile. She turned from the canvas almost angrily. This was where *he* had worked. She could remember him more vividly than ever, stood lost in imagining how it had been. The peace of the studio, the sitter usually reverent and co-operative for those few hours while she read in the sun chair near the window, time whittled to a caprice of brush-strokes, or the sharp *sshish* sound of the palette knife as he textured an image, blended a colour. The need rose in her sharply then. A terrible need. One which nobody every mentioned, which Marian always seemed to avoid. This was where they had occasionally made love, beneath uncurtained windows, bright in the sunlight yet tucked out of sight. This was where he was most himself, most the man. Within their own context, they'd had what seemed now to be infinite freedom.

Two weeks later, she'd seduced three men of her acquaintance. It had been remarkably simple, she discovered, as if they'd half-expected it, were well primed for invitations such as hers. But then, she reasoned, wasn't that what they assumed about a widow-woman, especially a young one. Couldn't the old peasant instincts always be relied on where a woman on her own was concerned? What exacerbated her regret was that it had provided no relief at all. Unsatisfactory couplings all three. The longing rose even more intensely, biting with a ferocity which almost frightened her. She made an appointment with a doctor. "Oh sex-withdrawal," he remarked. "Absolutely normal—you'll get used to it."

Marian was incredulous. "You mean you slept

with three?"

"I'm on my own now, aren't I?"

"I suppose so," Marian considered doubtfully, "but…do you really feel like it so soon after…I mean how can you feel that way now…?"

Did she feel like it. It was all she could do to avoid lingering on any attractive man she saw, even on the streets. She was more aware than ever of slender muscularity, of slim thighs, of fine, young skin. She was not merely hungry. She was famine-stricken.

"Best take it easy though," Marian warned confidentially. "I mean they might begin to think you're anybody's…" Again her voice faded as she struggled with the words, distaste and incomprehension etched on her features.

The party was three weeks later. "Bring someone," Marian had urged accommodatingly.

Lisa considered. "No. I'll come alone." She'd had no sleep for three nights, felt raw and sour as morning sunlight streamed unobligingly into her face where she stood in the hallway. She was beginning to get the picture. Her arrival with a partner would present no difficulties to a hostess. She hardened within. Let them sweat it out with the newly-bereaved woman. The woman on her own.

"OK. If you're sure," Marian had sighed.

"I'm sure. See you Friday."

She wore black. Simple black which plunged gently at the back. From her ears hung the old red-gold earrings which Alan had bought her in Turkey for their anniversary one year. Her dark hair was swept high in a pony-tail, revealing a long and elegant neck. She felt poised, yet strangely angry. They had travelled so many roads in those twelve years, had taken trains and planes, had lugged backpacks to bright, sunny places. She listed the countries mentally. Turkey, Morocco, Tunisia, Yugoslavia, Crete, France, Italy, Germany. The house was cluttered in a slight way with minor mementos, bits of carved wood, porcelain, camel-leather, rugs and blankets. She did not know why she had come to the party. Everything about her, everything she knew, was rooted in the past. But she greeted the husband of an acquaintance with a *bonhomie* which she did not feel, realised that she wanted to cause discomfort. She would do what they imagined and feared, what the limitation of imagination allowed them to see. Aware that some of the women would pity her, that she would have been the occasional subject of one of Marian's lunches, she knew also that tonight their sympathy would metamorphose into rigid suspicion.

Suddenly she saw him and demanded of Marian that they be introduced. Marian had drifted competently between groups of people who clustered together like constellations. Stars in their own heaven. And who was he? Dog-star Sirius, bright, bright, full of need and loneliness, attached to nobody, to nothing but a past. He was young-looking. Before Marian could do anything, he had approached of his own volition. Certain she hadn't seen him at any previous gathering about town, she took the initiative by telling him so.

"Bill," he said by way of introduction. He was slim, even bony. Almost immediately she noticed his hands. The left one was scarred below the knuckles, the skin around the healed wound smooth and sallow.

His hair was moppish, curls instead of the geometric square so beloved of men in their twenties. His watch was Sellotaped together and read five past three.

"How do you tell the time?" she asked impulsively.

"Time? Oh, I manage. I look at the sun." He smiled, shrugging his shoulders. She extended her hand towards him. He looked at it for a moment, and for a split second she thought he was not going to respond, but he took it and brushed it quickly and matter-of-factly.

A woman she'd never met approached. "'Scuse me, 'scuse me," she pushed towards Lisa. "Jus' wanted to say how…how terribly—" she struggled to form her words "—*sorry* I was about your husband, really sorry, really sorry."

Lisa murmured acceptance, dropping her voice as she always did when people spoke of Alan. The woman held on to her arm irritatingly. "If you're ever stuck y'know, if you ever need someone to chat to—must be hard." She removed the woman's hand in what she thought was a discreet gesture.

"No," she answered mutely, "it's not so bad now, but thanks for being so kind."

She smiled at the stranger, hoping she would go. Bill looked on, his expression intensifying. Again she caught her forearm, this time holding fast. Lisa knew the type. If you smile at them you've had it: they come on even more strongly, grow more invasive by the second.

"I know what it's like," the woman whispered wetly, "I know what you're going through…" This time she removed the hand more roughly than she had intended, and her voice was loud.

"Yes," she replied clearly, "I'm sure you do. Now thank you so much. Don't let me hold you up." Her back rolled with perspiration, resentment and frustration beating a rhythm in her brain, hands rattling the steel bars of a cage. The woman's face darkened as if it were about to become abusive. Her mouth opened and her eyes narrowed.

"Can I fill your glass?" It was Bill. Thank God, thank God, she thought, as the woman relented when he touched her elbow and proceeded to lead her across the room.

Lisa's legs had begun to tremble. Just the sort of thing she could do without. She swallowed as her throat swelled with self-pity, and tribes of unnameable angers assaulted. She glanced quickly around. Marian had heard the conversation, stood with a couple who looked casually in her direction from time to time. Taking her drink, she sat down near the door, where the night air swirled in soothingly. She turned her face towards the draught, unsure as never before, full of a torment that could never have been anticipated.

She surveyed the crowd with hatred. Threads of the conversation drifted towards her, "…badminton…ladies team…after a coffee morning…new exhibition in the Douglas Hyde." The voices rose and fell but there was no solace in the tide of sounds, only a gathering tempest that must surely strike. They were all obscene, herself included—dressed in bright leathers, animal skins, their arms, ears and hands heavy with jewellery, the men just as much part of the conspiracy, careful social animals, fenced-in wildcats who could purr smugly because they were well-fed, well-dressed, well-sired.

She jumped at the touch of a hand on her shoulder. "Sorry about that," Bill apologised. "Steered her back to the gin. A few more won't make any difference," he grinned.

"Thanks," she replied dully.

"No problem," he responded. "Not what you need I imagine. This is supposed to be a party, not a funeral..." He broke off suddenly, as if he'd said something inappropriate. They looked at each other for a long time. His face reddened. Suddenly her laughter exploded, and finally he laughed too, an easy humour in his eyes. He was an unknown quantity, a person actually capable of embarrassment. Nevertheless, after they exchanged phone numbers, she left early and alone.

That night she stretched out as fully as possible in the double bed, felt the chill corners of unexplored territory with her feet. This was how it would be, this was a sense of the future. A widow at thirty-five. Widow. The word revolted her, bounced tenaciously about as if forcing her to accept its implication. It reminded her of the spider, the one that poisoned its mate after copulation, suggested blackness, mothers of sorrow, women who would never enjoy a man's company or friendship for fear of what people might think. Widow. In the early Christian church they were a special class of pious women, who performed certain duties approved of by their elders, duties which kept them out of mischief, away from other women's men. Bill, she felt certain, may have thought he recognised easy prey. Yet he had done nothing about it. She shouted out in the darkness, swinging her fists back to the headboard of the bed, hammering till her hands hurt.

In spite of everything, she felt no different. Desire refused to evaporate with death. It would have been convenient had it done so, had all her lusts and wants gone down to the pyre with Alan's body instead of remaining with her like a malevolent inheritance, festering within, contorting her perception. Eventually she slept, aware that the birds had begun to sing, that the first buses were lurching down the road.

It was a mistake to mention Bill to Marian, even if unavoidable. "For God's sake be careful. You shouldn't take such risks."

"It's six months now. Don't be so pious."

"I'm not. Just worried about you...By the way I'm having a lunch next week, can you come?" she asked, changing the subject.

"When?"

"Wednesday."

"No, I'll be with Bill."

He had sounded surprised when she rang, but the light voice betrayed no displeasure. He was, if nothing else, curious. Marian picked up a magazine and flicked through it sullenly. Lisa smiled. Marian liked to call the shots. Without meaning to, she enjoyed an element of control in her role as chief comforter of the bereaved.

"Gotta go. Work to do at the studio."

"Alan's?" Perplexity flickered on her face.

"What was Alan's. I'm converting it. I'll rent it to a couple of artists. There's room for at least three— no point in having it lie there."

Younger than ever, she thought as she opened the door. He had brought her flowers. Carnations, spicy and aromatic, as if he knew. She would accept full responsibility. He had done nothing, made no move towards her. He stood in the middle of the hallway, awkward-looking, bonier than she remembered.

"It must be strange," he commented.

"What?"

"All this," he gestured with the scarred hand, taking in the whole house. "You're not used to it— by yourself I mean."

Simple words stung most, especially kind ones. She answered with a "no" that was almost a whisper. "Want to see around?" she asked lightly, in an attempt to recover her equilibrium. "I've lots of books," she added nervously. He nodded. She brought him through the house, from the black-and-white tiled kitchen with its scrubbed wooden table on which stood a chipped vase of lilac, to her workroom, and beside it what had been Alan's.

He was discreet, like a gentle but rangy-looking wolf that knows its limits. They ate in the kitchen, where it was bright and warm, and drank a bottle of red wine. Later, she felt the response in the pressure of his lips on her cheek but also caution, an unwillingness to make assumptions. It might not be a mistake at all, she thought, dimly recalling Marian's reaction the previous week.

They undressed self-consciously in the bedroom. "I'm scared," she laughed.

"Me too," he replied, stroking her shoulder. His body was smooth and supple, so beautiful it almost made her weep before they lay down. Then her arms and legs were full of his smoothness, his hairless body, his avid movements.

But just as she let herself go, no sooner had the

first moment of release torn relievingly, than it broke. The tempest. What she feared and anticipated. All of a sudden she was blinded by the wrench of memory. At first he misunderstood her cries. Gradually it dawned. She clung to him, clawed like an animal tearing the earth. Her mouth opened as she let out a long cry. It was a kind of primal grief. He made no attempt to release her, to be rid of her, but held on. He was tender and gentle. He stroked her hair, whispered in the hollows of her neck. Words that meant nothing in particular. But the voice was human and the skin was human.

The body was a man's, a kind man's. She caressed him again, and sobbed even more, his name, not Bill's, but the old name, the other name, the lost name that she could never utter again. Still he didn't move. Still he stayed close, his arms cradling her, his hands and mouth enacting a rite of consolation, drawing her on, bearing her as gradually she wept less and it was only when she had screamed the name twice more at the moment of release as it came again, that she let herself rage at him for having left, that she cursed Alan with serpentine venom. It was her turn to mollify the dark spectre, her turn to court favours of the unknown, to escort a sensed but unseen figure beyond the portals of desire.

Much later, they slept. She awoke in the middle of the night, felt him beside her, curled loosely in sleep. The chains had been sundered. Doors flew open, door upon door, leading out to a horizon, giving a sense of space that would not be dissipated. Somewhere in the distance, seagulls mewled. For the first time she was calm.

Every Day is Tuesday

High tide today. It batters the pier, flings kelp across smooth concrete, wraps it like a monstrous Medusa around the pylons. Kelp is dangerous. That muck-yellow sheen, saturnine, the spore-packed bladders waiting to be split by the storm. They will spill upon the sea today. Clouds are wrathful. Offence and insult invest everything.

People act as if nothing is happening. They ignore the weather, like beavers building a dam, while upstream the flurry and broil of their collective fate gathers. They don't realise who I am. If they did they'd change, stop this madness they call normality. Blasted hypocrites. I stand among them and they won't see it. Mother knew. That's why they fought. He couldn't stand it, banished her to the bedroom because of her vision. Mother, I will heal you. For your wisdom I will heal you.

How they talk! They don't know that I can hear. I perch in the nest of their heads, watch parasites hatch and feed on every nerve of their miserable day, rise through the skin pores, make them sweat with suspicion. Yes, they are parasites. They need these hatched thoughts, this perpetual babble, don't know that I know, how much I know. I sit at the window, contemplating. Watch that woman on the sea-front, umbrella buckled like smashed red fruit in one hand, wicker basket hanging on her left arm. Even today, she minces past at half eleven. Even today. Ignorant of what she carries on her left arm. The receptacle. I swing from her left arm, her left side, she actually puts me on the side of darkness, sets me swinging—sinister, sinistra, sinister, sinistra,—makes me fight her battle with the face of evil, day after day. Cowards. The lot of them. How they talk! And laugh. Look at that gaggle. Their laughter washes the discordance of their lives upon me. That they could ridicule me so.

No rest. The messengers stream in by day, by night. I need sleep, daren't risk it. They've hexed the child already, sent evil through the very bricks, lie in wait, in the child, for the day. They plan to spring when I least expect it. I shall master them, shall make them bow before me. They shall know my prescience.

I am not here to work like the drones, caricatures of men, with brief-case and suit, planned family, planned extension, the sculpted garden, their alcohol-sodden Delta mentalities. They cannot leave the house, the cell of knowing, and hope to remain uncontaminated. They invite risk by going to the city, the centre, to push pens for a few hours of the morning, lick arses and hope they won't be offered a voluntary redundancy, say yes-sir, no-sir, three-bags-full-sir, talk about breaking even, about net profit before and after tax or net depreciation, fiddle with words in hope that assets outweigh the spectre of liabilities. They're all liabilities as far as I'm concerned. They endanger me, knowingly. Someone must be sacrificed for their redemption. What do they care, sitting behind the pink crinkle of the money newspaper at lunchtime. Scared shitless. That the pink tower will collapse beneath them, that the fragile construct of their snivelling lives will topple plans for modest success, moderate family size, reasonable leisure-time activities, the great plan of the mediocre existence, of compromise, of meeting half-way, of probing the body of consolation beneath the web of religion.

They return in the evenings. Exonerated. Imagine they have earned rights as well as money. Back to the unpaid whore most of them house, breeder of children, that idealised romp in the hay they thought they had when they married.

Too much freedom, that's it of course! Men have ceased to be luminaries. The women educate themselves while they're away, and they're surprised when words like "fulfilment," "meaning" or "purpose" lace the evening meal, gird it with subversion. What purpose can they possibly have? We are their masters. They must know it. She knows. That's one thing she's learned. I—am—authority. It took a while, but finally she acknowledges it, recognises the mistakes of the past, the affairs, the extravagances, the wild nights when I was ill and the pair of them collaborated to put me away, to project a mutual impotence, their inability to face perfection. I must endure, carry all, assess the vagaries of keeping things intact, the vast, wheeling organism, the pulse-spot of the universe. I worry. I, alone, worry. I must keep it perfect. They can't admit that.

She still denies the affairs. Perhaps it's her pride.

Nobody likes to admit total error, to take responsibility for mistakes of magnitude. That I accept. But she in turn must accept me as her master, acknowledge my dominion over her, over them all, must love my access to truth. Mother saw that. He was jealous and he killed her. I knew it would happen. I had seen, even as a child. The voices would wake me in the night. I was immersed in whiteness and fire, in rings of sound, the first whisper and echo of truth taking me like a lover's halting touch. They guided me for years, brought me to strange places, to witness, in preparation for my work. How beautiful those voices. A perfect seduction of the spirit, a cohesion of affective and cerebral, and the joy of knowing, of seeing. I heard them clearly, vitally, and they brought peace and comfort. I could never have been like the others.

Mother tried to prevent the marriage. Sensed weakness in the woman, knew she'd find it difficult to love her master. Ah mother, you were wise and warm!

When I was eighteen, the voices increased, raised their pitch so that it began to hurt. The blue veins along my temples steamed with the pain of knowing. Yet pain was beauty and truth, and only this web of skin, of bone, of ligament, prevented me from transcending, for ever. The pitch of sound beckoned, told me about myself, reaffirmed what I'd long suspected. My day will come, will dawn victorious. They will bow their heads and feel ashamed.

The woman dislikes sleeping with me. The idea of what it means frightens her perhaps. She has served her purpose. She brought forth with energy, in pain, on our bed. I heard her screams. She lay alone and was seared by it. No doctor. No need in the cell, near the presence.

It was like the first day, when the firmament sundered and the solar system spun, the blue eye of earth opened, sleepy with newness, burning with ferocity in a jewel-like solitude. In that eye lay the life-forms, the saline properties that would bring the cosmos to fruition. How her belly grew rotund with the months! We waited. Every picture, ornament, plant, every stroke of paint, every architrave, was suspended, hung meaningless before the day her belly broke its waters and the child swam, amorphous and fish-eyed, water-crumpled, towards me. In a manner of speaking. I was not present. I have no taste for blood or the screams of women. It was all I could do to contain myself on the balcony while she yelled and blasphemed. But in that way, she served a purpose, perhaps the only one.

I know she takes medicaments. I've spied the foil in her bag, or in her jewel-box. She fills herself with preventatives, cannot look me straight in the eye when I wonder why the child has no brother. He was born on Tuesday. Since then, every day is Tuesday. She found that difficult to accept, but eventually she admitted that every day was, indeed, Tuesday, cried the delight of knowing it, screamed it for me. My ways are not her ways. It's difficult, yet she must accept. Tuesday, Tuesday. Every day is Tuesday. Choose-Day. And—I—shall—choose.

Occasionally, I become like the rest. I enjoy these forays into humanity. Something within quivers, grows warm and tolerant towards their imperfections and fetid trials, the bland routine of their lives. The feeling grows that I too am subject to those laws. Then she tells me that I should always feel that way. She is indescribably lovely, a woman of rare beauty, at the height of her powers. There is something in her eyes at times like these that I cannot grasp. They grow moist, yet she does not cry, does not crumple like a piece of overripe fruit, the way she might at other times. Her beauty is arousing but it also tugs at my tenderness for her. We might breakfast on the balcony, overlooking the sea, eat toast and marmalade, sup dark lakes of coffee, might touch, call to one another through our skins, hear echoes like the sub-aquatic sounds of lonely sea creatures. And think that perhaps it might be good to live like the rest, sense that the air around us is rivetted with a cool pall of contentment. And we look toward the bay perhaps, watch the morning boat cut obliquely through the silvered panel of the day, let what is realised, what is realisable, ride out, swathe the best of our love across water.

I remember what attracted me initially, years ago. We were in a restaurant. We'd chatted. The meal was over. Suddenly she rose to put on her coat, elegance and delight to mine eyes, her hair long and brown, face alert and good-humoured. As she stood, my eyes dropped to her legs. Then I saw it. Exquisite. The dropped hem. That small pucker, then the bit of hemline hanging loose, and a silvery pin dangling open. The feelings of tenderness it aroused were extreme. In all her co-ordinate ways, her quiet fastidiousness, here lay the sweet flaw of the trollop, and I knew that probably she wore greyed underwear, suspected that her tights were possibly torn and holey above knee-level. I did not love her for her efficiencies but for what I knew to be a rapturous humanity. This woman would not worry about matching socks, would not wash on Monday, iron on Tuesday, bake on Wednesday, sew on Thursday, shop on Friday. She would simply do what was necessary as the need arose.

But the voices came back, beckoned more strongly than ever. Contingencies, contingencies. I am a necessary being. What else could she do but subjugate herself to the plan? I must have order, require a perfect environment for contemplation. There is no place in this mansion for fallen hems, no room for pins holding things together. If I am to embrace all, I must have peace, the sibilance of order, must sense the spiral of infinity.

Naturally, because of the task before me, I cannot work. So she earns something small. Not outside our home. They'd get to her, use her as a vessel to bear those forces, herald them into the presence, like the Trojans. She stays with me and the child, attends to her duties. In the afternoons, she types manuscripts for the barrister in the next apartment. Even that sound disturbs me, but I have chosen and she must stay, for when the time comes I will need her. Sometimes I suspect that they're getting at me through her typing. That hammering, that concise, unrelenting pummelling impedes my clarity of thought, nulls it, defies perfect logic, breaks the pattern of continence. I sit here by the window when it rains, like today, or on the balcony when the weather clears, yet cannot escape the sound, the macabre metal voice, the stamp of metal on paper.

Every so often, she makes excuses, usually when she is cursed. When that happens, I forbid her to wear jeans, or anything tight, and she must sleep in the child's room. Women. They disgust me, they are an insult to perfection, with their perpetual flowing and ebbing and seeping. And their vast thighs, all that flesh, the ripple of fat, striation of muscle. You know that if they got to you they'd—unthinkable. But when I forbid her to wear jeans, I also give her a dispensation which means that for one afternoon at least, the machine is silent.

Mother never wore jeans. None of them did at that time. They knew their sin, had the courage to bear it in silence, to pay the price of damning perfection forever. They ruined us, with their bodies, their smooth skin, their prominences. Now they live by the moon, these sisters of Satan, because they threw thorns in the path of the godly, sullied man's knowing, stunted his strength.

After the voices, came the visions. The child was a year old. I chanced to look at him, found him suddenly invested. His face shone, his features transformed from the curve of childhood to a startling angularity, icon-like. Presence was there, that sense of inspiration, that immense sorrow of knowing. The pale face of the great spirit. My face. The luminary. The time had come, through this visitation. She resented it, of course, could not see it. Rang them, cried and stuttered a lot, and got them to come in a hurry. First the ambulance. I wouldn't go. I had seen truth. Then the police, all blue lights and politeness. They couldn't make me either—I hadn't struck her. Finally another ambulance, and this time they took me. This time, they sent Beelzebub's bullyboys, incarcerated me because I knew too much, because they resent my truth and will deny who I am. When I had quietened, after a month, when I stopped repeating what I knew to be true, pulled a clamour of doves back from the sky and started to act like them, they asked me if I would like to go home.

Fugitive in my own cosmos, how they hunt me. I have seen, my memory engorged with their futile attempt to grasp the lily, that white, pure, perfect truth. They killed for it once. Father did. His wrath knew no bounds when I transcended his authority. He lost her in an instant, dominion fell to the Son, and he killed her. Henceforth must I walk alone, wrestle their infidelity, their blindness, their waxed ears. Some of them talk about life being a joke in bad taste. When love affairs turn acrid, or friends betray, they whimper like pups and speak of black comedy or *la condition humaine*. Boosts them, I suppose. What else have they but self-deception? Two hemispheres, and years pass disputing the significance of a cleft in their fuddled brains. Man is right hemisphere, woman is left hemisphere. So it goes. Woman would, naturally, embrace the left. Sinister, sinistra. I have it all. Have grasped the lily, because it's of my creation. Without the contemplation, computations, without the constant attention to detail, they'd all die. If they knew that! Would it make a difference? If they knew the day of their deaths, that it is inscribed on the tablet that swings, invisibly, from their necks?

When the time is right, they'll be ripped by the roots from their beds of despair. The adulterers, the buggers, the sodomites, the harlots, the homosexuals, the abortionists. Women who leave their children, who usurp authority by working outside their domain, who forget what virtue is, and the joy of humility—ah yes, the sisters, the abortionists! Out with them, lest they destroy the mansion.

The signs are everywhere. Yesterday it was the dove. It flew close, rested on the balcony rail, as a sign. Now the mark of the dove is everywhere, for those with eyes to see. Even her slippers lie beside the bed, angled slightly. They are invested with the dove. Further confirmation. She will not see it, works sullenly, silently, her eyes deadened by the briar of ignorance. If the child cries, she rushes to soothe him before he disturbs my meditation. She has learned how to live with me, partially, and she fears my wrath. Each evening she locks the knives away, permits no medications to enter the apartment, excepting her own illicit store. To protect me, she says. She forgets that I will always be here, even till the end.

I am not of their world. Sometimes I wonder if there is hope for humanity, any redemption from the scourge and pain of living, any reprieve. Even for me. The burden is more crushing with each day. Long ago they cut me down, tore me apart, and he who killed took no blame. They sheltered him in the bloodied garb of a plausible religion. They refuse to leave me. I cannot leave them. They say they love me. Paint me, sculpt me, write, wear spiked chains on the insides of their thighs in my name, build layer upon layer, their golden, moneyed desire on my effigy, set it aflame with the frenzy of power. It must be hate. They treat the cosmos like a tennis-ball, bounce it, batter it, try to make it yield perfection, compassion, affection. They sell their souls for affection. Baton my name and call it love. I call it hate.

They seek me. The final death to be re-enacted. Give them half a chance and they'll do it. So I wait. Within four rooms. I have chosen. They shall not attain me. They may mark my effigy, sunder it enviously, may dance with the ancients, praise or blame, ascribe sin. I have seen. I know. I wait, alone.

The sea has calmed. We contemplate, eye to eye, grey to grey. I shall sit on the balcony till dusk, when she makes me eat. Eating gets more difficult because it disrupts the plan, insults contemplation. Yet if I retired for even a second, stopped in my tracks and said "Enough!", the great elliptical wheel would grind to a halt, the giant reds, the pulsars, asteroids, Phoebus and Demos, Jupiter the wrathful, Saturn (evil influence, no harm if it went,) brittle Mercury, and blue-eyed Earth, the whip and whirl, aspiration and desire, would crumble calamitously, dissolve, seep to the seabed, to the saline phase. Back to the drawing-board, as they say.

No dove today. No sign.

The tide is restless, whinnies gently. Even the kelp fingers at shingle, to reach me. The pier is puddled, the sky torn, lachrymose. Lights prance along the coast, hold the black bulk together. Head flares with wisdom, with knowing. My benevolence will keep them safe, even the transgressors. In the absence of doves, her slippers are before me. I pull the caul of sleep on the world, let them be, let them rest in innocence. The clamour whirls in my head. Wingbeat and buffet and aerial dove.

Snow

People drifted in pairs or clustered around the open doorway. It was stiflingly warm in the function room. Buses roared past the open windows through which spirals of sleet spat. Earlier in the evening Rawson had assembled the magazine in neat stacks. To his pleasure, it was selling. Jimmy made a thumbs-up sign from the makeshift cash desk. He nodded in response, unsmiling. He Richard Rawson poet and novelist, had got his act together and produced *Obelisk : The Irish Short Story Magazine*. He checked his watch. It would soon be time for the official launch. They would stand in nominal reverence most of them while he uttered the requisite words, performed the rites with an appropriate degree of seriousness, tinged perhaps with laconic humour, urged them to buy the mag and spread the good news thereof.

He looked anxiously to see if Gabriela had arrived. He needed her presence, felt himself confronted by a hazy blur of garments and half-familiar faces. Like it or not, he'd have to have his eyes tested. Either that or he was more nervous than he could admit. Suddenly, his stomach lurched as he recognised her back, heavy coils of red hair falling about her shoulders where delicious knobs of fine vertebrae held him in thrall. He made an effort to control a fondness of glance, to temper it with fitting disinterest, to stifle the desire to stare, drink in, adore. Only a week had passed since the day in the mountains. It seemed like eternity.

Anne approached with the three boys in tow.

"Nearly ready, chick?" she asked.

"Yes, sweetheart," he said with all the feeling of an automaton.

She bore her public smile, the social one which proclaimed their unitedness. The very sight of her irritated him this evening above all evenings. The heavy set of her jaw, the manner in which she linked his arm, announcing by that gesture, their long-standing union as husband and wife.

"You've never met O'Leary, darling, have you?" he said, a trifle eagerly. He steered her toward Tony O'Leary, where he stood tall, puffy-eyed, affecting suavity in a loose cream jacket. He was editor of *Argus*, known for his incisive comments on the poets of the 1950s and his penchant for detailing a civil and sensitive family background.

"Tony!" Rawson greet jocosely, "Glad you could make it. Have you met Anne and the kids?"

"Dick!" O'Leary responded in an exhalation of cigar-smoke. "Great stuff—so ya finally awrganised yourself, hah?" he drawled, ignoring Anne. Bastard couldn't even extend a hand, thought Rawson. He needn't have worried. Anne stripped her teeth and smiled, said something faintly witty that drew from O'Leary a response which was either a half-snarl or a half-smile.

"There's someone I must see, angel. Be back in a tick," he said, slipping off to the left. They deserved one another conversationally. She who could rabbit on about causes and the Left and socialism, would pin-point the real issues for O'Leary whether he liked it or not. Christ, but he was sick of her woolly-headed brotherhood-of-man nonsense, marches to the Dáil, sit-ins, lockouts, campaigns and petitions, the numbers of which seemed to mount with every year.

He joined Gabriela's circle. The irony of it caused him to smile. Ostensibly the gentlest of creatures, she seemed one unlikely to attract a gregarious circle in such a public setting or hold anything of interest to frantic socialisers and yahoos. Yet she was the very core of any proceedings, no matter how trivial. "Richard darling, congratulations!" said Annette Kermode, embracing him. "Well done, Dick!" said Jacko, her husband, slapping him across the shoulders. Gabriela murmured vague felicitations, as if she barely knew him. He accepted their words graciously if not ecstatically, feeling them to be his due at this stage of his life, not just because he was forty-six, but because he had had to set the whole thing up with minimal resources and no funding from the Arse Council, as he called it privately.

"Gabriela—Levi, isn't it?" he made a pretence of being unsure of her surname.

"That's right," she replied demurely.

"I'm Richard Rawson. How are you?" he said easily, shaking her large, smooth hand, the hand which had precipitated an interior earthquake only a week before. Rawson, the able communicator, the man with a *bon mot* appropriate to any occasion, who could put people at their ease, identify and encourage new talent—the Lord knew it was thin on the ground.

"Quite a crowd here tonight," she said.

Annette and Jacko weren't listening.

"Indeed. Gotta get the punters in somehow" he sighed knowledgeably, enjoying the game to the full.

"The booze always helps," he added.

"Best of luck with it anyway," she said, and he knew she meant it.

Her face was deadly serious, but the grey eyes betrayed a miniscule trace of warmth, a carefully revealed shade of intimacy. He felt almost sick. Sick with love for her. His stomach churned with tenderness and desire. Jesus. He was lovesick, and at his age. If Anne got so much as an inkling, she'd ridicule him mercilessly, would scream and row for days, terrorise the children in their ever-fragile peace and tell him that there was no fool like an old fool.

"Get yer ass up there, Rawson, and launch the bloody thing and stop flirtin' with innocent young girls, would ya?" said Jacko over the top of a pint.

Rawson looked at her again, tossing his head in Jacko's direction as if to say, would you listen to yer man!

"All right Kermode," he bantered, "I'm keeping an eye on you." He turned towards Annette and winked. "Just you watch that fella."

It was best not to hover, in case that by some grotesque fluke, Jacko was on to him. Wouldn't do to be caricatured in the *Phoenix* as a pre-senile, over-the-top vulture, slavering lasciviously at anything in a skirt. They would never understand that it just wasn't as simple as that, would have had to be in love to comprehend the accompanying madness. And they weren't—most of them. He crossed the room, stopping to chat with various old establishment sages. Humour them for God's sake, Rawson, he commanded himself. He attended to all *en route* to the rostrum and microphone. An affable "Hello" here, a "Glad-you-could-come" there. Keep them happy at all costs. Gabriela had once said that he conveyed an impression of over-plausibility. It was the only way he knew.

Fionn O'Boyle from south Armagh, approached like a man with a mission. A complete non-runner, thought Rawson as O'Boyle wished him luck gloomily, and added between his teeth that the odds were against the magazine's success. A pox on you, Rawson fumed inwardly. A pox on the hungry, still-miserable nation whose people had failed, where tunnel-vision was the outstanding quality of a collective journey down the Swanee. O'Boyle's introductions at readings were renowned for their earnest and fun-deadening aura. A sermon on the mount preached from a molehill. Rawson smiled to himself, hoped it was an appropriate response to whatever O'Boyle was droning on about. He recalled O'Boyle's last launch. A trio of musicians had been assembled during which the cellist and oboe player scratched and honked discordantly for an hour before O'Boyle had read through his teeth, a heavy northern drawl lending feyness of tone to his words. Himself and Anne, on tolerable terms that evening, had brayed with laughter in bed afterwards. It was the best belly-laugh they'd had in months—so much so that it initiated a day's reconciliation—before they tore into each other again. Shortly afterwards he had been interviewed by Gabriela for a small French quarterly. It was an interview which had turned into a prolonged yet hesitant conversation.

He recalled again the day in the mountains which followed, many meetings later. It was cold and frosty when they stopped at a delicatessen in Donnybrook and bought beef and salmon sandwiches and a bottle of white wine. He talked excessively as they drove out the Stillorgan carriageway, aware of a light sheen of perspiration above his lip. The talk, he told her later, was the only way he had at that point of saying, "I love you." Once or twice other cars blew their horns at him. He was culpable, he knew. Careless driving. He could hardly keep his eyes off her as she sat there, mufflered and gloved. Occasionally she'd comment on something he'd said. She could disagree without being combative. *Terra incognita.*

There was snow on the mountains, but he kept driving, elation at being alive governing every move. He felt strangely purified, free of dross and disappointment—the deathly attrition of the years.

"Shall we park here?" she suggested, buttoning her red coat.

He adored the sight of her in that red coat! They had arrived at a fork in the road, locked the car and began to walk. As usual, he succumbed to his self-imposed pressure to be amusing, regaled her with the tale of how he and Anne had once visited The House of Peace back in the sixties when a group of primal therapists were having a get-together. As they passed one of the rooms, some guy within had screamed the most godawful scream, as if his leg had just been sawn off. Gabriela had laughed as if it were really funny. That pleased him. People rarely laughed genuinely, so rarely responded to anything any more. He felt old, knew the privilege of being with a woman like Gabriela. Barely thirty, responsive and warm. She was an exotic voyage, a new departure. Every cliché rang its truth in his mind, in spite of his being accustomed to the assertive doyennes, dogmatists and modern courtesans who had, in recent history learnt how to put pen to paper, order their thoughts and recreate the female experience. She was, she had said, crazy about him. Unbelievable, he had thought, overjoyed. They walked through the snow for an hour—it could have been more, or less—feet breaking the firm whiteness. Arms around each another, they wandered randomly. Once, she stopped.

"I have to pee," she said.

He had turned his back and walked on as she squatted for a few seconds.

"Let's go somewhere private," he said later, as they headed for the car.

"Isn't this private enough?" she said.

"I need to be alone with you," he said, reprimanding himself inwardly for sounding shallow and predictable.

"You are," she said, "But..." she hesitated.

"Yes?"

"It's so powerful."

There was a slight hiccup in her voice, a brittleness and tension which made him want to gather her in his arms, to protect her, if such were possible. She bent forward and wiped the condensation from the windscreen with the back of her glove. He drove a short distance. They were silent. Finally, they came to a turn-off, what looked like a disused entry to a farmstead. He was more nervous than he could ever have imagined himself, knew every muscle to be taut, noticed his hands were moist. He directed the car down the gravelly slope, then pulled to a halt. The whiteness outside was blinding. It reminded him of the effect of having stared at the sun for too long, when the cornea reacted by producing a negative image. He wondered if they were mad, out of their minds, stuck in the middle of nowhere in the freezing cold. "Will you be able to shift the car out of here?" she asked.

He hadn't replied, had leant over to kiss her and as he tumbled into her felt his senses expand.

It was time. He mounted the rostrum, forcibly evicting Gabriela from his mind. As he tapped the microphone he noticed Baldwin enter, Baldwin the loathed, who used every launching to give himself a plug, to generate a sense of supremacy and preciousness about his own press. He had told Gabriela about Baldwin that day, said what a complete shit Baldwin was, what a bog-wog, who floated up to town once a week from the depths of his boghole in Kildare. Rawson had ranted, knew his account, based on old rivalry, to be abusive and subjective. Gabriela listened, her eyes judging but not harsh.

He braced himself. It was important that his presence be felt, that he bear down on the consciousness of those who had gathered in the hotel. He realised, looking down from the rostrum, that he despised them. Yet they were his own kind. Ranks would close, arms would be linked when it was imperative that they, the artists, band together in the face of a culture which was ready to view them as peripheral.

"Friends," he began in resonant tones.

"Romans and countrymen!" somebody quipped from the back of the room.

There was a ripple of laughter, in which Rawson shared. He was warming to the task.

"Friends," he repeated more sombrely.

This time there was silence, except for rustling around the door, which creaked open and shut. The windows had been closed. Traffic-sounds hummed distantly.

"We live," he paused as if to reflect, "in a culture which is anti-creative, which places little value on the work of the imagination, sees no link between the world around us and the interior space of the mind." He paused again, to lend weight to his words. "Between the world around us and the cosmos. It is a culture which too often rejects the invitation to consider, to reflect upon affinities and infinities."

He stopped to take a deeper breath. His heart was pounding. Anne was looking around, hawk-eye picking off various targets to the right or left, potential enemies about whom he would doubtless hear . Head like a bloody doorknob. The children were not with her. He scanned the room, saw the boys help themselves to juice from the drinks table at the back.

"We all know the fate of journals in the contemporary world," he went on.

"Hear! Hear!" called a woman near the front.

"It is a fate with which journals have always met.

Many perish after the second or third issue, because there is no money to float such enterprises; and the public does not care."

They were listening. He would pace himself.

"But we must make them care. It is our task—our burden if you like—to stir the consciences of a people whose primary concern is to pay homage to the great Janus-head of Relevance and Mammon."

That got them. Some faces looked alert, others posed intelligently. Gabriela was watching him, her expression closed and serious. The thing was, he believed it all. "The collapse of such journals and magazines is, of course, no reflection on their promoters—rather—", he began to prod the air with his forefinger, knew that he was heightening the dramatic scenario, "—it is the shame of a nation which does not respect the force of its own psyche..."

At the back of his mind he thought again of O'Boyle: messed-up projects, squabbles with printers, hotch-potch promises made to aspirants which would, eventually, be broken; an inability to manage money which reinforced the multitude of prejudices already held by the public. He was setting his own standards in a perhaps too public arena, but it was his turn to shaft, his chance to reply. "—and this magazine will succeed where many have failed," he heard himself pledge, as had so many before him.

"I hope you will buy a copy tonight. Read and enjoy the best living writers which our country has produced since the flowering of the late nineteen-fifties." He looked pointedly at Tony O'Leary.

"This—is a feast !" he proclaimed, "Celebrate, my friends!"

The applause was, on the surface of it, rapturous and immediately satisfying. Hands plumped down on his shoulders.

"Great stuff," he heard, "Keep it going," and "You're on a winner, Dick." He needed a drink. O'Boyle and Baldwin were having a go at one another. He knew by the way Baldwin was standing, arms folded defensively across his chest like the bloody gremlin he was. Jack and Annette joined him. Someone handed him a whiskey. "Jays, ya missed yer vocation, Dick," Jacko grinned, his way of expressing support. His eyes searched for Gabriela. Again, he needed her, but urgently, as if his life depended on it. Then he saw her, chatting with Anne. He was both startled and amused at the treachery of it.

He knocked the drink back and went to get another, remembering the day in Wicklow, playing and replaying every image, selecting, re-examining, handling each moment with a sense of discovery which could not be forgotten. They had eaten the sandwiches, drunk the wine, shared the bottle in long, thirst-quenching gulps, began to laugh and continued uproariously until the windows of the car steamed up completely. They grew warmer, began to kiss again, showering each other with tenderness. Jackets were removed, shirt and blouse unbuttoned in haste, and he still sat behind the steering wheel, half-paralysed with surprise, as she opened his belt and unzipped his trousers. They lay for a long time, grew chilly. He drew his coat over them. Outside, snow had begun to fall.

He had lain still, his hands stroking her head

occasionally, stunned in a happy state of renewal, as if the steady approach of a way of life he dreaded, the conditions and posturings of age, had been temporarily halted. And more. It was not so much a rejuvenation as a union. Suspended in a snow-shell, he was aerial, alive as never before.

Curiosity and the yearning to be near Gabriela got the better of him. He shouldered his way past Baldwin, O'Boyle and their acolytes, face fixed and beaming. The two women ignored him initially, beyond glancing up as he stood there. Anne was giving Gabriela a dose of travellers tales. He moaned inwardly. The other woman's reserve betrayed neither boredom nor unease. He heard the familiar phrases. Turkey again.

"...well I mean the taxi-ride from Dalaman to Fethiye was un-be-lieve-able!" Anne exaggerated, "The driver could hardly keep his hands on the wheel, kept looking back at us and smiling. Well, it was probably a huge scoop of a fare for him. Those people have it rough you know..."

"Yes, I know" said Gabriela, "I lived out that way myself for a year."

Typical of Gabriela. Understatement. His wife's expression altered. She had, Rawson surmised, taken Gabriela to be the gobdaw she herself had once been. Now she listened with heightened interest.

"Oh? Where?"

It was a challenge.

"Baghdad."

He knew all about it, watched as the other woman made a quiet impact, spoke knowledgeably and quietly about the problems of being a freelancer in the East.

"I see..." said Anne. She sipped a drink reflectively. "Yes, well—" she hesitated, "I've never actually worked in any of those places. It must be a totally different experience."

"It is. You can't really imagine the difference between being on a holiday, even a long one like you had, and earning a living in that part of the world."

Rawson held his breath as his wife's face took on the vestiges of mild admiration. She had obviously decided that here was somebody with whom she could relate. In no time at all, she'd try to wheedle Gabriela's address out of her and would, likely as not, arrive unannounced for Sunday lunch the following week. Anything to avoid cooking. God, she embarrassed him. He had to get her away.

"Darling, can I interrupt, just for a sec?"

He realised his face was frozen in a ridiculous smile.

"Yes, angelkins, what is it?"

"I have to check on Jimmy at the door. He might have cash-flow problems," he said in mock-confidential tones.

"Could you see if Feeney and O'Connell are in the other bar? I'll have to introduce them in a few minutes."

For a moment, he thought she'd create difficulties. Instead, she turned benevolently towards Gabriela, insisted that she accompany her in hauling the contributors from the bar. Damn, he thought.

Suddenly, as they moved off through the crowd, he was swept by pity for his spouse. That she, whom he had once loved, should engender nothing but spite. The feeling was replaced immediately by resentment. He wanted to weep, to lay his head down somewhere—anywhere! He sensed denials, yet knew there had to be some release. If all else failed, he thought, if the magazine collapsed—unthinkable after all his work—but if that happened, dare he hope for something far greater, a prize, the undreamt?

The old weariness threatened to creep over him again. Images of the past ten years rose unbidden. In a fraction of a second, he evaluated his literary worth, thought of the jealously guarded opus, the master–piece which could deliver him—finally—from the niggardly world of hacks and botchers of great art. Anne, his most castigating critic, had never seen it. Only Gabriela had read fragments, the better chapters. He had hopes of finding an English publisher. He watched fondly, catching a glimpse of her again. She beckoned then, a cold, pure breeze, whiteness of fallen snow, untrodden, unsullied. Such a comfort, he thought. Such a comfort.

Baldwin moved across the room with reptilian slowness and lifted a copy from the stand. Rawson observed as he handled it, fingering through the pages with apparent distaste, then replaced it and left. O'Boyle at least would take a copy. Incompetent as he was, he still had the generosity to support the enterprise. Rawson's mind idled over the problem of distribution. He had to ensure that bookshops which had already agreed to take copies would continue to do so. Having paid his contributors at the going rate, he was, furthermore, broke. He poured himself another drink as he waited to introduce the rising stars who were there to read from their work.

Come In—
I've Hanged Myself

The social worker had described him as fairly typical of his age group. "You know the sort of thing I mean," he drawled casually over the phone, "a bit mixed-up, needs somebody patient to take an interest." And Lorna, eager to appear cooperative and parental, had replied, "I know, I can imagine," when she could do neither. Missing his parents. Father in England. Mother in a psychiatric ward. She made a point of not tidying the house on the day of his arrival. An air of spit-and-polish would inhibit him, she thought. He'd want to relax, feel at home, as if he belonged. No point in creating a formal sanctuary, a sacramental atmosphere. Feeling slightly appre–hensive she left the previous day's papers tossed on the floor of the sitting room and decided not to arrange fresh flowers in a vase in place of wilting carnations.

When they opened the hall door, the social worker was hearty. He grinned, pulling on his beard as he introduced his charge. "And this bod here is our Martin!" he enthused with a flourish of the hand. "Go on shake hands with Lorna and Luke like a good man," he intoned encouragingly. They shook hands. Lorna heard herself respond brightly, cheerfully, to the mumbled greeting. Her head, unexpectedly alarmed and unsettled, whirred with attentiveness. He was pathetically ugly. It had nothing to do with dress or build. He wore black and grey, the current A-bomb garb of despair and redundancy: black trousers which ended mid-calf, a grey shirt under a black tunic. A chain belt hung round his narrow hips. He was much what they'd expected. "Come on in," Luke beckoned, sounding hospitable and easy-going. Fatherly. "The fire's just on—it'll only take a wee minute to warm up."

They chatted, the first awkward moments mitigated by mugs of coffee. Mugs, not cups. Deliberately chosen for the occasion. One part of her responded superficially. Another wrestled with uncertain feelings. The boy looked around aimlessly. He could only be described as unfortunate looking: his hair was wiry and short, neither brown nor blond but pale and neutral. His face was ravaged with acne, the skin waxy, the cheeks and chin pocked with volcanic swellings, angry pimples, and the scars of half-healed eruptions. His jaw showing the primitive angularity of a young male. Here and there, wisps of hair sprouted. His eyes were pale blue, ringed with a pig-like pinkness.

They'd painted the walls of his room a plain buff, in case he wanted to put up posters. He shuffled from one foot to the other, sheepish and tongue-tied.

"D'you think you'll be OK here, Martin?" she asked.

"Yeh."

"If there's anything you need you'll let us know, won't you?"

"Where's the jacks?"

"Oh of course, nearly forgot," Luke half-apologised. "This way." The chain belt clanked all the way across the landing.

All young people liked chips. Burgers and chips, Luke had suggested. So Lorna chopped onions, minced round steak, added herbs and bound the lot with egg in big juicy mounds.

The chips were home-made. They sat down together, feeling awkward.

"Are you hungry, Martin?" she asked, certain of culinary success.

"Yeh."

"Oh—you can wash your hands at the sink before you begin, if you want," Luke interjected. They'd agreed on this in advance. No direct requests yet. Certainly no orders. You achieved more by example.

"I washed them half an hour ago."

"Fine. Fine," Lorna said quickly, her look meeting Luke's. She handed the boy a plate. He eyed it uncertainly.

"I don't eat chips."

"Oh?" she queried, surprised. Waiting for him to say more. He didn't. Began to pick at the burger.

"I don't like pepper in things."

"Oh well, we'll get you something else then." She made to remove the plate. He stopped her.

"It's all right. I'll eat it this time." He sounded almost aggressive with his deep and half-broken croak.

"Are you sure? It's no trouble." She laughed uneasily. She was uncharacteristically nervous. He poked at the burger, cut it finally and ate a mouthful, looking straight ahead. This had to be what a blind date was like. No inkling of what was in the other person's head. No clue to their wants. And natural parents could imagine things. Could trace things, mistakenly or not, to genetics. But this was *tabula rasa*. He lifted his fork solemnly. "I'll eat this today. The chips make me skin worse. I like them. But that's why I don't eat them."

It was as if a light had gone on. She found herself admiring his blithe reference to his skin, to the distorted plumage of his face. He had declared his cards, in a manner of speaking. Or some of them. Had told them something about the sort of person he was. She was flooded with curiosity. All things in time. The rest of the meal passed easily. She and Luke tried to tell him about their friends and their friends' children. Their relatives and the Sunday visit in a few weeks time.

He liked toad-in-the-hole, he told Lorna suddenly, one Friday. "And shepherd's pie. Me Ma used to make things like that when she was feelin' up to it," he remarked.

"I'll do shepherd's pie tomorrow," she said, delighted at this reference to his mother. Things were shaping up.

"No. Do whatever ya were goin' to do," he said hastily, in a wavering baritone voice. Of course, she thought. How stupid. How insensitive not to realise that to cook a favourite meal would perhaps make him lonely.

She knocked on his door that night. To say goodnight, even though they'd already done that. "Yeh," he called expressionlessly. She pushed the door. He lay on the bed, arms behind his head, staring at the ceiling. The radio was on. They'd get him a better one, with headphones. And tapes perhaps. He liked AC/DC and Cindy Lauper. "Good-night," she mouthed, unwilling to disturb him. Unwilling also perhaps, to deal with the uneasiness he aroused in her each time they attempted communication. It was apparently simpler for Luke. No complications. A bland directness. Mutual. Devoid of complexities. What could they really say about what went on behind that face? That pock-marked face. Sometimes, it seemed as if he wasn't really with them. Like a strange bird, an alien creature moulding itself to an existence where everything was cruelly unfamiliar, where the other denizens were made of paper. Hollow where he was full. Useless at meeting his wants. Or perhaps *they* were the aliens.

He grew sullen. More truculent in manner. Determined seemingly to thwart their efforts. He despised routine. The night before the Sunday visitors arrived, he stayed awake, listening to music. That did not disturb them. More the notion of a wakeful and slightly hostile presence stalking around downstairs. The next morning, Lorna asked him if he did that often.

"What?" he muttered blankly, staring into space.

"Stay up all night."

"Yeh."

She would be patient. This was the sort of thing you got.

"Can't you sleep then?" she continued casually, pretending to be more interested in the cookery book she held in her hand.

The boy was silent. Just when she'd decided that he was going to be perverse, he stirred.

"I can think better."

"Oh. I see."

Don't tell me we're going to have four months of nocturnal philosophising, she thought. In the summer too. He should be out and about during the day, getting some air. Still. Fairly typical behaviour, when you thought about it. Attention. He probably did lots of things for attention. They'd have to ignore the exhibitionism. Make him feel important in other ways. Build up his self-esteem. Life makes you what you are.

Later that morning, she tried to involve him in the dinner preparations. But he dawdled uninterestedly, arms folded. Watching her. She had to admit that he was tiresome. The old understanding between herself and Luke vanished in his presence, so bent were they on pleasing him. Nothing pleased him. He was a gigantic puzzle, brooding and mysterious, who foiled their anxious attempts to find the missing piece— some anodyne to a mutual and mounting chagrin. Her patience was dwindling steadily. He'd been with them two weeks.

"Right Martin," she announced briskly, trying a new approach, "you can set the table—you'll find cutlery in that drawer and the crockery's here beside you." She smiled matter-of-factly. He didn't smile back. Just looked. Instantly seeing through her facile adult psychology. But he went to the drawer and got out the cutlery.

Dinner was a disaster. The vegetables were passed around while Luke sliced the lamb. The boy stared at his plate, pale-eyed. Somebody—Luke's father, she thought—started grumbling about unemployment. It was an easy topic, the sort of thing about which everybody could rave, feel hard done by. They bantered agreeably for a few minutes over the clink of plates and cutlery. "What do you think, Martin?" Luke's mother asked gently.

"About what?" he muttered, not looking at her.

"Well," she hesitated, "about unemployment and that, all those young people like yourself who'll be leaving school in a few years and no jobs for them— what do you think's going to happen?" He put down his knife and fork as if about to make a statement of policy.

"I don't know and I don't give a damn," he spat.

There was a brief, uneasy silence. Lorna cut in.

"Right, you don't give a damn. Very original, Martin," she smiled.

"I'm not tryin' to be *original*," he scowled, mimicking her.

Her face flared. "More lamb please," Luke's father said, clearing his throat.

"The streets are going to run red." They all looked up startled by the sudden announcement made five minutes later.

"What you were askin'," he gestured at Luke's mother with his knife.

"It's going to be a blood-bath in ten years." He helped himself to another piece of meat.

"However do you mean?" Luke's mother asked quizzically.

"Don't have to explain, streets are goin' to run red—I don't have to justify that to anybody," he growled, head swaggering in the glow of their acute attention. Somebody—Luke more than likely—sighed.

They talked in low voices as they did the dishes.

"A lot of it's for attention," Luke reasoned. "If we ignore it he'll stop eventually." Lorna disagreed.

"We have ignored it and there's no change," she fumed.

"He's still acting as if he were doing us a favour by being here—it's as if we're idiots—can you imagine him when he goes back to school?" She paused to pull the plug, and dried her hands angrily. "Carrying on about us: how we behave, imitating us!"

When they went into the sitting-room, he was rolling his own cigarettes. As if he were alone. She watched him, fascinated. Totally self-engrossed. Oblivious to their presence as he fiddled with the flimsy paper, his shoulders hunched, head and neck protruding forwards. Sixteen. She reminded herself of their obvious advantages. And his disadvantages. Insecurity, fear, immaturity, no experience of a loving home. And an appalling appearance. Pity was the last thing he needed. She felt so little affinity with him. Because he gave nothing. Went through the motions of being cooperative. If he enjoyed anything, he never said. Presumably he'd never been shown how to express pleasure. Maybe there'd been none to express in the first place. No. It was up to her and Luke to make the effort. Go farther than half-way. Beyond the median line of compromise. Possibly nobody had ever gone beyond what was necessary on his account.

"Don't flick ash on to the carpet, love—there's an

ashtray beside you." He glared at her. The family left early. They departed quietly. Luke's mother would probably phone the following day.

No doubt he saw them as set in their ways, committing over and over the mortal sin of middle-class adulthood. Dinosaurs with pea-brains, who knew nothing about pain, loneliness, anguish, who were eternally sure of themselves. Yet his own behaviour was so familiar. Predictable. The very thing he objected to continuously. *Come In—I've Hanged Myself*, proclaimed a sign on his door. Another, on the bedroom wall, read: *Life Is Like A Shit Sandwich*. Everything about him was an indication of internal furies, an unsubtle display of nihilism and youthful ennui.

It came to a head the next day. Luke had gone shopping, unable to persuade the boy to accompany him.

"That's wimin's stuff," he announced to Lorna.

"In this house it's everybody's stuff," she replied firmly. "You can go next week, Martin—we all take turns here."

He rolled his eyes heavenwards, curled his pale lips down defiantly, helped himself to one of her cigarettes.

"Are you out of pocket-money already?" she asked. He lit up, contemplating the smoke. "Nope," he muttered.

"What would you have done if I'd said you couldn't have one?"

"I'd have taken it anyway."

The little shite. He knew how to rise her.

"Look," she began reasonably, "we've tried to

make life pleasant for you but all you do is throw everything back at us…as if…as if…"

"I don't owe you anything," he shouted, hammering the table with his fist. A hint of violence that made her stomach curdle. She studied him carefully, lighting a cigarette herself. Distant and assessing. He was hateful-looking when he was angry. He returned her gaze, challengingly.

"Martin, the one thing you do owe us," she began softly, determined not to raise her voice, "is consideration." She gesticulated with the lit cigarette, "And that means making an effort—some attempt at playing your part—and none of this 'I-don't-give-a-damn' nonsense. We only want you to feel at home…"

Suddenly he rose, pushing the chair back noisily, stubbing the cigarette so roughly that it broke in two.

"Nobody could be at home in this…*Kip!*" he bellowed. He might as well have hit her. "Well, if that's how you feel Martin you've only to say the word; we don't want to hold you against your will if you're not happy; if you can do better elsewhere…" Echoes of her own mother, years ago, when faced with mutiny. Her voice was even, controlled, in spite of the hurt. To her surprise, his face flooded pinkly.

"You don't really want me here at all," he croaked. Her face dropped.

"Ya couldn't have yer own kids so ya got me on trial, like y'can hand me back when me time's up, forget all about me."

He paused momentarily, like a hurricane building up to its peak of destruction, the veins on his neck bulging.

"I don't want to be stuck with a pair of cranks who

couldn't have their own; you're batty, that's what you are, with your books and music," he goaded effectively. Despising. Determined to stab where it hurt most.

"Anybody that listens to operas, ah—whatever ya call it—has to be up the creek. A header. That's what you are," he hissed maliciously, pointing at her.

There had to be some redemption. Something positive had to come out of this. A reason she could connect with, some moment of salvation that would heal them both. She would ignore most of it. She would. She would. She tried to control the nervous tremor in her voice. But she could not let him see her reduced. Perceptive boy. She'd call his bluff. "You're right, Martin," she tried to sound blasé, unshockable. "We couldn't have our own kids. And you're right again. You are second-best. In fact, come to think of it, you're third-best, because we couldn't adopt either." He shrank visibly. But she couldn't stop. Knew she was hitting back. Meeting him with even greater maliciousness. And she didn't want to stop. "That's if you go around measuring things. We don't. It's nothing to do with third-best. You're you. You're nearly grown up. You're not a child even if you behave like one. We thought we'd like to have somebody like you live with us. We have lots of space. It could be handy for a fellow…and we're not trying to be your parents." Her voice jerked. He started to shriek at her. "But y'are, y'are!"

The perversity of it dawned. The real want. But, by then, she could not relent. "Look honey, I wouldn't want to be your Ma for all the tea in China. Don't delude yourself," her voice hard.

Luke came in then. Looked expectantly from one to the other, sensing an airing of emotion on the normally neutral domestic channels. "I hate you, *bitch*!", he roared, kicking the chair as he made for his room. Crying. She was crying too.

It was fifteen minutes before she could say anything comprehensible. It poured down her face. They couldn't get this right either. Came across to the boy as a pair of stuffed shirts. Tied up in reproductive tensions and what they had transmitted to him as "culture". Antiques who knew nothing about anything that mattered. Who would soon be extinct. Acting Mr and Mrs Bountiful and *understanding*. In reality, they understood nothing. They had nothing. He'd stripped them, bared the hoarded pain of years, the mask she wore to conceal it. Like some wild thing tearing at flesh. And she was no better. Had kicked back every bit as hungry. As defiant. Had reaffirmed the image of self-loathing and repulsion which he harboured towards himself.

Unforgivable.

They decided not to disturb him when he didn't appear for tea. Let him cool off. She began to think of the sign on the door. Supposing? Would he realise they cared? Before they went to bed, she knocked on his door. Silence. She tried again. A rustling sound. Then silence. She knocked a third time.

"It's open," rasped a half-fledged voice.

He didn't look at her. Lying on the bed, smoking, the air curling grey-blue. Flat out, locked up in himself, impenetrable as a piece of steel. Wrap the tender part up. Bury it like a broken bone. Let it fester.

"Martin?" Silence. He exhaled.

"I'm sorry. Just called in to say…that I really didn't mean…never let the sun set on your anger…" She was incoherent. Touched his shoulder. He flinched.

"There's food in the fridge…if you're hungry…" She left quietly.

Went to bed, doomed and impotent. They were a right pair. Clueless. And the boy hated her. Clearly. The venom he packed. The blind energy of something unexploded, which could shred their civilised masks to ribbons, expose the raw nerve of need. Headers. That's what he'd called them. Called *her*.

She wanted to crawl away. Anywhere. To find peace. Somewhere safe. Where the effort of doing the right thing wouldn't always backfire in her face like a badly-primed pistol. A place of reason and salvation. Some people had it easy. She drifted towards sleep. So easy. All fell into place. Two point five: average family.

Halley's Comet

I t all began to fall apart when you did the secretarial course. The golden carrot held out during months of Pitman and pee-bee, tee-dee chay-jay, or rattling valiantly on the typewriter, was a job in Guinness's. It was difficult to feel enthusiastic about that. You weren't interested in typing letters about stout.

When you went home at weekends, you'd set up the telescope and squint at the moon to see how the *Mare Tranquilitatis* looked. Inevitably, the same as before. Would ponder for the umpteenth time a grey and cratered star whose identity constantly eluded you. It was a dull-looking little piece of rock, north of Orion's Belt. It was silent, like everything else out there, wonderfully so. Compensated for a week of learning the art of subservience and willingness at the Holy Scourge Academy of Smiles and Politesse.

Then it was back to Dublin on the express, with a weekend case, every Sunday night along with other hopefuls from this or that college. You were all terrified of your shadows but eager to get out, to succeed, to be all-rounders both at work and socially. The priority was to get there. Fast. The terrors, naturally, were never admitted. Once the bus had pulled out, a standard activity was to share out the packet of *Gauloise Disque Bleu* or *Gîtanes*, and spend much of the journey in the fermented blue haze of cigarette smoke, hands poised, heads tilted contemplatively.

After the secretarial course, came the architect's office. Your brain still pulses to think of himself, grovelling like a periwinkle or some horny crustacean, before every nun or priest who wanted to build a school. You stayed three months. During that time, you descended gradually into Hades, had most of your dreams cracked (if not shattered) as you attempted to comprehend the phone system, his personal habits, his partner's halitosis, and the great mystery of PAYE and VAT returns. A veritable baptism in the ways of the world: how to crush the spirit (almost); how to set it reeling into the abyss of *hic et nunc*, close a door which reads "No Exit" on it, confine it where everybody is tied to a giant pound note, eyes waxed over with Unguent of Mediocrity.

Your worst fears about the world were confirmed, totally. The problem with this commercial sanctuary was that you saw no *point* to it. Any of it. Made the fatal mistake of thinking that you were wrong, or odd, or obtuse, and that *they* were right. Like an addict in need of a fix, you took to carrying the book of basic astronomy in your handbag. Always liked the pictures and illustrations anyway, the lucid explanation of what a rainbow was—something you could never touch. It was comforting to understand how those colours were comprised, even though you knew vaguely that the sum of things beautiful equalled infinity, spiralling on in the soul for ever and ever.

At ten you'd calculated that you'd be thirty-two when it returned. Decrepit. Too old to appreciate it perhaps. Nevertheless, you'd set about getting on with life, nurturing an anxious hope that you wouldn't have lost interest in such matters by the time you reached thirty-two.

You'd seen it as a sort of interplanetary relative who returned every seventy-six years from her travels, a little more burnt out at each visit, more experienced with every orbit, and indescribably exciting. A bit like the returned Yank of the fifties, but more exotic. This was an explorer *extraordinaire*, the David Attenborough of the galaxy that returned reliably, unwavering, bright and brilliant, from each voyage through the unknown. What was more thrilling, more devilishly alluring, than the unknown?

Life proved damnably ugly. The city was hostile. Masses of people bouncing along the top of Dawson Street at lunchtime, rushing blackly against you. The Green was to be avoided at all costs. You did not know how to react to the whistling and clicking, to the all-approving but violent male gesture of the raised and clenched fist. You perfected the guise of the poker face. Gradually, it dawned that you'd been living like a peach-coloured glasshouse orchid, safe and unchallenged in the country, ignorant of the city's rip-roaring teasing and rivalry that was as natural as anything else in life.

This was life. This was what went on. A bit of skitting around for a few years. Then the hysteria of falling in love, of "going steady", a Christmas engagement which might include a watch as well as the ring, worries about pregnancy ("It sort of—

happened—like—I didn't mean it to—"), and marriage the following March twelve months, before the end of the tax year, in the event of those worries being allayed.

That really took the biscuit. How could you possibly be in love—really, passionately so, and even think of marrying in March in order to save money. Then there'd be a baby and a christening, then another baby and another christening, *ad infinitum*, *ad nauseam*. Because again, it was natural. Reason had nothing to do with it. And you worked, if you were a man, to support this crazy system. You actually went out and kept it going, contributed by the sweat of your boredom and the disintegration of your suit.

What was crystal clear was that you'd have none of it. Ah Daredevilina, how brave, how noble, to relinquish nothing! And you mulled occasionally over Halley's Comet. That would seem pointless to them. There was no way of convincing them it wasn't. Nothing rational you could say which would prove that this meant something. In the overall sense of things. You just knew it did. It was *out there*, driving on at unimaginable speed, bursting forward, burning up gradually with its own energy like the sun, leaving a long, bright tail in its wake which would refract beautifully, like ten rainbows, if the upper atmosphere was moist enough. You had to see it, when it returned from the yawning vault of infinite possibilities. Because some day it too would be gone, and in the meantime, you would enjoy its fiery mien of strength and eternity.

It was one reason for living anyway. You'd be there, telescope set up on the hill above the house, would have your glimpse of the mass of ice and dust you'd fallen in love with as a child. Because, in a way, it was to be a monument to your mortality, to the surviving of life and its full-frontal attacks.

The architect had a habit of sucking on his teeth. It drove you crazy. He'd do it standing behind you as you typed up something he wanted "urgently", a certificate for thousands of pounds which you could imagine him proffering obsequiously to the reverend client. His very presence turned your fingers to butter, oiled them as if to spite your desperate efforts to appear competent. Appearances were everything. You thought of the comet. "You're a great little girl," he'd say, grabbing the sheet and giving your shoulder a squeeze.

One afternoon, he rushed in, grey in the face.

"Liz. The bank's been on."

You looked up from the wages book.

"Someone has drawn a six thousand pound cheque on the office account—" He spoke jerkily, paused to slide his hands through his hair. You must have looked vacant. He started prancing. "The stub, Liz, the stub—who signed for it?"

You rummaged through a drawer, the word "someone" branded in your mind, took out a cheque-book. The wrong one. Your fingers fumbled uselessly around again. Your stomach felt queasy. So this was what a premonition felt like. Eventually, you opened another cheque-book. Flicked through the counter-foils, knew you wouldn't find the God-saving, all-absolving one, for £6,000, initialled neatly according to sacred instruction.

He cleared his throat.

"Well Liz?"

Kept looking at you. Jesus, he thought you'd helped yourself. He badgered gently but resolutely, convinced of one explanation. Could you explain the missing cheque, the unfilled counterfoil? You couldn't, you replied for the tenth time, humiliation making you speechless, disbelief bringing verbal ineptness. All the while he ranted, asked if you realised the seriousness of this, if you possessed a cheque-book of your own.

Then his partner arrived back after an extended lunch-hour pink-faced with Friday afternoon *bonhomie*. It was sorted out in seconds. He didn't apologise. You went up to the bathroom, slowly, and threw up.

After the illumination of those months you prevailed on your parents to send you to university. The pieces still didn't fit. This was just a different angle. Still, in spite of the exhibitionism, the brave debates on mighty issues like contraception, divorce or women's liberation (usually one of the three, rehashed each time so that it appeared to be a different motion), you spied a glimmer at the end of the tunnel. You began to feel the breath of the old inspired thought and met other visionaries who could not knuckle down nor stomach the pill known as Average—ones who had enormous pride and sometimes talent to boot.

German literature was full of it. Oddballs; misfits; romanticists; springtime, life-loving rams, who tangled head-on—those who dared to say and do the wrong thing, pleasing nobody, although sometimes they pleased themselves. The speculative nature of those pages. Every preponderance—every predilect-ion towards the bizarre, the difficult, the confused or troubled was contained, it seemed, in the mind of the Teuton. And this comforted, like a balm. Sweet and aromatic. Was a golden light beamed on your face, undeniably precious.

Still ten years to go till it returned. You no longer dog-eared the pages of *Pocket Astronomy* nor poured the same energy into the idea of life *out there*, no longer yearned towards expansion and absolute duration, or certainty.

All the same, you'd be disappointed if the sky was cloudy. Because this was a once-off. If you didn't catch it then, secure that intangible in your thirty-second year, you'd have missed the chance. It seemed unlikely you'd be around in 2052, the elixir of eternal youth not having been discovered. More than once, you'd found yourself humming a song which went "Is This All There Is?", having found your most recent experience of life to be flat, grey and devoid of effervescence, devoid of that seductive call to match the rhythm of being. Yet sometimes, for a few seconds, you found yourself in tune with the world and didn't have to bother about the telescope or take rambles through forests or talk to the dogs in search of a bit of peace and coherence.

Nevertheless, the notion of the importance of seeing it, like something written across the evening sky, or at dawn, like Elijah, prophetic, never left. But the prophecy eluded you. What would it mean? What was it saying? Had it a meaning, or was this something you'd imposed to suit the workings of your own twenty million grey cells?

Later still, in Heidelberg, Herr Prof. Dr. med. von Steinbock waxed enthusiastically about the search for meaning. This was marvellous, you thought, applying yourself to the task of translating his lectures into accessible English, picturing yourself at the forefront of psychoanalytic progress, at the hub of the unrelenting battle against the soul's dark night, as he addressed the World Conference on Violence. Your undauntable vanities. Light would spill into the blackest recesses.

After a year, he invited you to accompany him for a weekend "zu einer Konferenz in Salzburg". How come, you asked, premonition rising like a fever.

"Ach Fraulein Elees-a-bet!" he laughed coyly, "Sie sind eine sehr intelligente Dame—das müssen Sie schon wissen!" Damn you. Damn you. Damn. Damn. Damn. Kraut.

After that, you never wore your backside out by staying too long in anything. You'd met all the shysters, neurotics and sexual deviants by the time you were thirty, attracting them in the first place because you were prepared to listen to them. You'd avoided most of the anathemas that once seemed stacked, poised cruelly in your path, the real Hades and all its ugly portents ending the day you left the architect. You were still free to enjoy the comet, to still want to see it, which was more than could be said for many of your prematurely disillusioned acquaintances who were either exploring the labyrinth of the monogamous relationship or beating their brains out being career people, those for whom coping with life on earth was a bewildering and wearing trial. You were still waiting for it, in spite of life's normal quota of Disasters of Grand Design. But you balanced it. At thirty, you still felt eighteen. Thirteen. Even ten. Retained the capacity to gape, to be intrigued by something, in the way people used to when they got their first television. You'd managed some of it your own way, without relinquishing all to the righteous hiss of society.

All that remained was to see the comet. You'd do the Dance of the Sacred Volcanos if the sky was overcast; if the earth's natural processes came between you and it, between you and this brief distillation of your life, your efforts to rise above the fatigue which life can generate. There were billions of you simmering away in the same ancient pot, wrestling with memories and injustices, instincts and pseudo-rationalisations. Seeking a future. You'd heard echoes of the rhythm, had seen your way to some coherence. Perhaps you were meant to be slightly off-beat. Perhaps that was your purpose. Or was it function? No. Purpose hummed on the horizon, as sure as sunlight, and you needed that telescope, might need it always.

If the sky were clear it would be beautiful. You'd been ready so long, eager and waiting for years. Hoping for a velvet sky, blacker than black, the air taut and expectant, like pulled silk. When it came, you'd be there, telescope poised, the camera set to click at eight-second intervals. It might be something quite ordinary, when you consider the mediating power of adult perception, the crass tendency to reduce everything to its meanest value. But you liked to imagine it as a fiery ball rising on the horizon, brilliant with power, balled urgently in orbit. It would leave a dazzling tail, like the mark of a prophet, not warning, but signalling. Rejoice. Celebrate. Something that might make people stop and look. Or was that too much to expect?

Still. It might come like Elijah, not out of clouds, but from the depths of the black universe, and would bring the kinship of other places, the mighty sense of not being alone. Of movement, of evolution, of life to infinity.

The Estuary

After Saturday night confessions we'd go fishing on the estuary. We spoke little during those few hours. The important things had long been said. It was more a matter of learning to keep the boat from drifting ashore before we were ready, of making peace with uneasy winds that rushed to the open water, a great soft gush of air from the south wrestling with the more persistent one that swept down from Carlow and Kilkenny. "The guardian wind," Davida called it, the wind that parleyed with the river all the way from its source, ghosting it, an invisible agent that watched over its ancient force, then let it take chances with tides that wheedled around the estuary.

It always had to be at night. Always a Saturday too, when there was little chance of being seen. And the pubs were always full. Who, after all, would have accepted the necessity of our friendship? Who would not have condemned?

Kate claims to have always known, by the way we sat at the marble-topped table in the pub. "People who aren't allowed to do anything else let their knees make contact," she says. She also adds that my white collar didn't amount to anything, concealed nothing;

all this by way of letting me know what an astute judge of social behaviour she is. Generally I opt out of such conversations, the nit-picking and navel-gazing which she requires every so often, just when I imagine that being away from the place, that living here near the border, has changed everything. It's good to be free of what I freely chose and was impotent to change before I met Davida—polite obligations, the necessity of my presence at every dog-fight and do, the benison of raised hands, whether it was at bridge or whist, or opening the new community hall. It is liberating not to have to listen any more, as when my ever-open ears allowed professional access to their fretting, their rapacious need to confess every Saturday, scrupulosity driving them.

Kate and I, ten years later, two sons later. She cannot let go, refuses to let the past sleep, continues to blame where no blame may be.

"You'll always be a bloody priest!" she spits every so often.

Then I start to shout, grow angry at the first inkling, intolerant of her constant picking and snagging, like a terrier pulling at the limb of a dead animal. "You've still got priest's hands!" she'll add when she wants to really madden.

It's the stupidity of it that provokes, if anything. Once last year I almost showed her what my hands were made of, what *I* was made of. I didn't strike. But I knew and she knew that it was merely the chance remnant of control which prevented me. Perhaps it was her expression. She stood there, about to leave for school, brief-case in one hand, taunting me. When I finally snarled in rage and lifted my right hand, her face betrayed the flicker of instinctive fear which only a woman possesses. It was the slightest thing, but I felt ashamed. Cowardly. In a flash I remembered the train of bruised faces, broken collar-bones—even one fractured skull—all the beaten-down women who had made their way to my door when I was in the south. And oddly, I recalled one night after fishing with Davida, when it was warm indoors and our hands gradually softened. It was the moment when I knew I no longer cared, that I had changed allegiance. And remembering, I fell to my knees before Kate, cut to the quick by my too ready humanity, by hers.

One day, perhaps, I might eventually feel like a Monaghan man, whatever that means. It's so different up here, the chat is still strange. Some of them know. They may even know about Davida. These things have a way of being relayed throughout the clerical network, where there are too many lonely men with nothing to do at night but drink and gossip. And local people have a peculiar facility at ferreting out what are perceived to be the juiciest morsels of the past. Generally though, they're fairly circumspect. And from a practical point of view, it has all helped. The job interview was merely a formality, the reverend father assuming that even if I had fled the fold, I would at least possess the prerequisite standpoint, could be relied upon to respect the general ethos.

By now Kate and I are part of the school furniture. People sometimes remark how wonderful it must be, working with one's spouse. We shrug our shoulders helplessly. How can one possibly respond? There are times when we avoid one another, comically observed by colleagues. It's remarkably easy in a school. There's always a meeting of one kind or another, at break-time or at lunch-time; so that if one wants, it's quite possible for a whole day to pass without having as much as brushed against one another on the corridors.

I first met her on a school corridor. It was a Thursday in March, the day I usually made my rounds of the local schools. I was standing by a window which overlooked the estuary, that point where the river suddenly looped out towards the tidal pool. As I fixed my few papers, rehearsing whatever I was going to say to the assembled fifth-years that day, there was a clatter. Looking around, I saw that she had slipped on the stairway. Half-horrified youngsters stood about, at a loss what to do as Miss Devereux sprawled beneath a heap of essay-scripts. But she rose quietly, efficiently, with the minimum of fuss, told the children to move along to class and thanked one or two who handed her the scripts again. Just as she had reassembled herself, she saw me. Probably I was smiling. "Smirking" was what she called it later. Our relationship started on a note of good humour. It was easy and relaxed compared to the frantic meetings with Davida. I had applied for a dispensation by then, lived in waiting for good graces from Rome.

Women, women, women. Living with one is almost as difficult as living without. Almost, I say. Kate cannot forgive Davida for having existed. Cannot forgive me for having loved—if that's the right word—another before her. She is—I have to say it—the type of woman who when younger, thrived on the notion of the virginal priest, the scent of what was supposed to be unattainable. Kate despised fishing, still loathes anything which smacks of intensity and compulsion, because she associates those qualities with Davida and me, regardless of the intensity of her own resentment, her love and her hate.

There are little lakes up here. Every opportunity for the fisherman to follow his dream on narrow, glacial tarns nicked between the eternal hills, surly lakes of infinite depth, you suspect. Once or twice I've gone out alone. She pushes me to it sometimes. All she has to do is to start untidying the past again, trying to rummage through my silence, for me to go out, slamming the door after me. Up here it's so different. Everything is harder, it's true. The people and their accents, the tone of voice, mean-looking hillocks and icy black lakes. The last time I went out on the lake, I felt weary of battle. I sat for a couple of hours, didn't lay a hand on the oars most of the time; it was so calm there was no need to battle with wind or current, as I would have had to do out on the estuary with Davida. Nothing demanded and nothing given. I sat smoking, thinking. She is not forgotten. Nothing ever really is. I looked around but there were no distances to aspire towards, just bristling hedge, colonial-looking laurels and rhododendrons which tumbled around the lake edge. Everything here seems inward-looking: nothing to see beyond the immediate hills which crowd in on all sides. I grew despondent that evening, felt indescribably lost, felt that I had betrayed myself somewhere along the line.

About once a year—around the time it happened, early April—Kate asks if I miss the old life. She is full of clichés. *Once a priest always a priest. A spoilt priest. He left because of women.* The answer is unproblematic. There are no unplumbed traumas with which to struggle, nothing Christ-related which seems in any way abrasive. I found my Christ, stumbled upon it passionately in the wide-armed form of woman. Found it first in Davida, whose suffering was invisible, whose daily Gethsemane was lived in her laughter and verve, the fierce-cut proud laughter which she wore like a suit of armour when most ill, when the seasonal Furies came to visit.

Confidences are a trial, an opening, an invitation really. I often think about the beginning of it as I walk through the uneven streets, past vegetable stalls, or across the square where a church spears the sky with its no-nonsense testimony. I remember the evening it first happened, when Davida and I chanced to agree on something trivial, something significant enough nevertheless to be opposed by the others in the group. It was after a parents' meeting that I had chaired, which had had to do with fund-raising activities for improved play-school facilities. By that agreement, whatever it was, we opened the way for confidences. Fatal. The future contained in a look that concealed its smile.

I went back last year. For all sorts of reasons. I was, you might say, homesick. There were people I wanted to see.

"Tell them I was asking for them," Kate said tersely. Her jealousy is so finely-honed that she cannot permit herself to accompany me south any more, refuses to stand by when I most need her. It's as if she's testing, wants to pit me against Davida even yet, senses betrayal in every absence. There's no convincing her.

"It's your problem, not mine," I say nowadays.

"What the hell do you mean it's my problem?" she demands angrily.

"You refuse to be responsible—for yourself..." I suggest. "You don't want to accept that I care for you, how deeply I..."

She shrieks, infuriated, "That you *care* for me, as you put it—care, care, care!" Her face is red.

"Now you're talking priestspeak, Con, bloody priestspeak!"

The rows are verbally violent, furious, and I'm as bad as she is: I can't help avoiding the word "love". The fact that I don't use it, is—even yet—misunderstood by her, although I've explained why. It's not that I can't say it, not that I don't feel this composite of tenderness and lust and unnameable things which people refer to as love. She should know better. What has love to do with anything, when we have so impenetrable a carapace of civilisation, our urges so over-psychologised, so labelled? Life goes on, I tell Kate. People will have their way, whatever that way is. Humanity insists on expression, like a river seeking the sea, thrusting through an estuary, over silt and seaweed, across mudflats, unstoppable in the need for access to something greater than itself.

Nothing had changed very much when I went back. Perhaps that's my illusion, the tendency to think that the past is intact. People remembered me, of course. They don't forget priests so easily, especially priests who are no longer priests. The village pub had been extended, was full that evening of holiday-makers, Germans and Dutch who came to fish along the south coast or on the estuary itself. Conversation was light.

"You've become an Ulsterman, Con," somebody said.

"Would ye listen to the accent of himself!" someone else remarked teasingly. Part of me was diffident, conscious of how much I wished Kate were there. To confirm, as it were. To establish us as a pair before the all-seeing eyes around me. The place became loud and smoky, the smell of spirits, the bar, pint-glasses and sodden beer-mats becoming oppressive. More than ever before, I believed that Davida was gone, that Kate was correct in her resistance. I chatted until well after closing time, tried to answer their innocent questions about life in the northern county. Was it very bad up there? Were there a lot of Provos in the town? Some didn't know that Monaghan was in the twenty-six counties.

Around one o'clock in the morning I drove down to the estuary once more. This was what it was all about, where it was all about. The locus. A curlew called from the other side, a long, piping call. Love. This was love. To be by the estuary again. I knew it, with the certainty with which I had known Davida. To feel oneself part of a place, for whatever reason, as much a part of it as the river and the sea, or the wind, an element at the heart of its own place, careless of any other existence beyond its own. That was why Kate sometimes hated me. I was—unpossessable.

I left the car and strolled out along the pier. The moon was well up from the sea, had turned the quietly slapping water into a phantasm of itself. Yet it was real enough. Lights flickered on the other side, and the old fort was silhouetted greyly in the distance. Every so often the water plinked, bubbles rose. My eye followed a train of them. The bubbles. I recognised the exact spot where I'd stood the morning they called me out when they dragged the estuary. I had kept my hands in my pockets, fists closed, my black clerical anorak pulled well up around my ears to keep out the cold. It is something not to be forgotten. Kate knows that, cannot rest easy as long as she feels that she might not have been a first choice, that she cannot fight the good fight with the living, must settle for what she can neither observe nor control. She has taken well to the northern county, relieved to be as far away as possible.

I stood there awhile, remembered how one of the divers had signalled to the men operating the drags. "Easy now. We've got something here." The silence was one which screamed at the clouds for release and I couldn't provide a release, dared not. I was aware of men standing about as I bent over her. Somehow I controlled my face, took in the bloated skin, the open mouth from which a piece of seaweed tendrilled, the dead, fish-eyes. Around me, birds were singing, that peculiar crying type of singing which they work to an ecstasy in early spring.

The men urged me to say the last rites, called me to be a priest. It was the last time. My hands moved quietly in the air, marking a blessing somewhere between her and me. In that moment, they didn't know what they were doing.

The Inheritance

"**A**re you quite sure it's all right?" I repeated, wishing to convey my caution, my respect for her way of life. "I could always come next week," I ventured.

"Not at all, not at all," Marie interrupted. I could picture her at the other end of the line, smiling, meeting me every inch of the way with her consideration.

"After all," she laughed, "you must be keen to see the place after five years." Then, half-probing, half-anticipatory, "I don't think you'll be disappointed."

I set out at noon the following day, calculating that I'd arrive in the hills by half past two. That would give her time enough to do whatever she usually did. Part of me resented her in advance, felt brittle, even fearful. But the knowledge of such sentiments made me all the more careful not to upset the new owner. The decision had been ours. Cassandra and I had sold out, taken an apartment with Manfred, and gone to live à trois, as they say. Our new dwelling was large and airy and, I suppose, fashionable. We were relieved to be no longer lonely, and my paintings were selling.

Yet part of me was still a spinster: it persisted in spite of accolades, of some limited fame and financial security—in spite too of our much-vaunted relationship with the sculptor and the gossip-column snippets about our allegedly revel-filled doings. She lived now in the place where we became spinsters. Where that other part of me loves spinsterhood even yet, hearkens to it. Despised word. But not for me. To be solitary, even if sometimes lonely, is not the contemptible state it is commonly thought to be. There I produced the work of my controversial "Red" phase, working in the yard or on the rumpled lawn, at any hour of day or night. Not just painting, but being painted; beyond myself or reason, wholly absorbed as something vital and unique made its way onto canvas.

I took the avenue in bottom gear as was always necessary. It was more overgrown than ever. I became immediately excited at the prospect of this orbital re-entry to the world where I became the person I am. I turned the first corner, then slowed suddenly. Sunlight hit my face through the windscreen where originally I would have been in the shade. The beech trees had been uprooted and an entire hedge of laurel and dog-rose had been scooped away. In its place was a path of terracotta tiling. I braced myself inwardly. A succession of platitudes and plausible remarks raced through my brain. It's their place. None of my affair. What do you expect? Tempus fugit.

Marie had obviously heard the car, because the door opened as I lurched up the last curving stretch. She smiled at me from the distance, holding a baby on the crook of her arm, then stepped out followed by a Pekinese as I pulled up. The dog yapped furiously as I got out.

"Arianna!"

"Marie!" Simple invocations by way of greeting. We embraced in a pseudo-affectionate way. "It's lovely to see you again," she said, all welcoming. "You've no idea how quiet I find it." She coloured slightly. "Oh, I mean, if anyone knows about the quietness…"

"Yes, yes," I cut in, eager to assuage her awkwardness. "I know just what you mean, Marie." I closed the car door. "It does tend to be rather solitary, doesn't it? And of course, you're from a large family as well. You must feel it all the more greatly!" She nodded and made a face, receptive to sympathy, all antennae on the alert for information, news, the presence of human kind. She hadn't changed much in the five years, had the sort of skin that other women would refer to as "well-preserved" in fifteen years time.

"Goodness," I murmured politely, as she ushered me through the hall. "It's like going back in time." They'd redecorated, of course. She pushed the kitchen door. A tall, dark-haired girl was ironing a shirt. "This is Maisie…she comes in every Friday to help me out." Maisie looked up, curiosity on her face. "Maisie, this is Arianna, the friend I told you about, remember?" We exchanged greetings uncomfortably.

The kitchen was completely altered. The old wooden cupboards with the faulty catches had been replaced by a floor-to-ceiling affair in pine, with old world knobs and curves. A matching wine-rack—full, naturally—stood where our old radio had been. Instead of the long wooden table, there now stood an eating area not unlike a bar in a hotel, pine-topped and gleaming. One would have to sit sideways at it in order to approach one's food, I noted.

A series of floral prints were mounted in groups of four. I recoiled mentally at the spectacle, a straggle of pieces of blackthorn, rowan, lesser celandine and belladonna. Tastefully mounted and framed. But trite, positivistic, literal. "I see you've noticed my prints," Marie remarked, jiggling the baby automatically. "Justin bought them for my birthday. Aren't they gorgeous?" Once more, called to pass judgement in the form of an expected compliment. I had long since foregone the habit of tolerating bad taste, of uttering considerate comments about the wisdom of choosing this or that colour, pattern or theme. Life manages to invest us with enough placebos and contrived consolations. "Very tasteful," I remarked nevertheless, thereby running the risk of patronising her. The problem of diplomacy has always perplexed me. At least with Cassandra, we both knew where we stood. I used an upstairs room when the weather was cool, would work quite contentedly near the window, below the skylight. She, on the other hand, had converted the old larder at the other end of the house, downstairs, into a workroom. I could scarcely hear the rattle of her typewriter.

Every so often, we'd get on one another's nerves, partly from a sexual frustration of months standing. We'd then get deliberately drunk. Blotto. (Rarely suffered hangovers because we stuck to brandy.) We'd bawl obscenities at one another out on the lawn, throw newspapers or toilet-rolls, even wrestle. The more insulting it became, the more cathartic the effect. Meanwhile, our neighbours further down the hill, would have heard the screeching, and in no time at all the locality would be aware that the McGregor sisters were, once more, "at each other's throats".

We had moved into the lounge, as Marie called our old dining-room, to drink coffee and nibble at cinnamon-sweet fruit tart. It was difficult not to gape transfixedly at the brass canopy which ran from fireplace to ceiling, replacing our tiled Victorian affair with the mahogany mantle. Lumps of coal glowed electrically in the grate. She followed my stare, as I lingered over the past, winter evenings when the fire was lit early, the sparks all shift and glow, sap frothing from resiny logs. "Coal is so dirty, don't you think?" I replied that I tended to prefer an open fire. "Of course," she answered, stuck for a rejoinder to this minor point of difference. I tried to listen. Perhaps she was hungry for company. "It's a bit lonely, you know, with Jussie working on the new road beyond Mulla." She hesitated, unsure how far she should commit herself to confidences. "He's always out, morning, noon and night." She paused. "The workmen rely on him too much. They're likely to phone here at any time of the night."

"Yes, it must be difficult, and with children to look after too," I sympathised. "How many have you now?" and I realised that she felt uncomfortable and inadequate. "Four," she shrugged. "The others are at school. This wee laddie was a mistake."

I pursed my lips. Mistake. The contrived helplessness of it all. She looked up suddenly, as if struck by an idea. "Would you like to see your old room, Arianna?" I sat up from the cushion on which I'd lolled. "Why not? That'd be lovely!" I replied, longing to charge upstairs two at a time and burst through the door of my workroom.

We might have been old friends, we moved so languidly, taking the stairs with slow familiarity. Upstairs seemed brighter than I remembered. She opened the door to the room. A new door. Obviously this was now a young person's private lair. Posters everywhere. A portable TV. No longer the great double where Manfred and I had lain but a pert single, quilted and cushioned in pastels. The wall where the Rothstein portrait had hung now bore a large poster of a straddle-legged man in the process of unzipping an all-in-one suit. I averted my gaze, looked out the window, trying to sound absent and pleasant at the same time. "Well," and I forced a grin, "you've certainly left your mark on the place." I hesitated. "Of course, it's a little strange, bizarre even, to stand in this room again." That was a mistake. Bizarre. She wouldn't like words like that. They would make her feel inferior, have her imagine that I was affected. She responded slowly, although not as I had anticipated. "Yes," she almost drawled her assurance now, "it must be peculiar. I'm sure neither of us ever thought it'd be like this. I mean, with me living here and you somewhere else."

I turned, ran my hand casually along the dressing-table by way of concealing the mute anger which had risen in my chest. Mahogany veneer. "Indeed," I remarked evenly, "one can never anticipate one's long-term needs." A pause. She was waiting. "We haven't dismissed the possibility of moving abroad for a while. Of course, it depends on a number of factors." I wouldn't admit my need of the house; I had to show her that I was unfettered, that her alterations meant little to me, a mere curiosity perhaps. "Oh? Really? Where?" she gasped interestedly, perhaps seeing this as a prelude to some insight on the workings of the arrangement between Cassandra, Manfred and me. "Well", I bluffed, "we're not quite sure yet. Depends rather on the response I get in New York."

"Oh I see," and she nodded as if she understood. I was determined to punish her, somehow, for the crime of territorialism. She lowered her head towards the baby, obviously at a loss. "Do you hear that, baba? We have a famous artist in the house!" We both laughed uneasily.

"Telephone, Mrs Temple," I heard Maisie shout. Marie stiffened expectantly. "I'll take it up here," she called out. She gestured at me to stay put but I shook my head vigorously and motioned with my hand to show her I was going down to the garden.

The view from the doorway was as soothing as it had always been. A wide, almost horse-shoe shaped lawn, fringed by limes and beeches. The land beyond that sloped sharply to Tongs Lough. I could see the broken pier from where I stood. The lake shimmered coldly, although it was mid-afternoon. It lay enchanting and glassy, green and fronded around the edge but treacherously bright and deep towards the centre where the sun now soldered it. The town children, Marie among them, had always feared the lake. It was reputed to be full of ghosts and dead men's bones, and if you swam out too far you were likely to be caught by the ankle, dragged to an icy death in the clutches of Wee Menlo. Cassandra and

I had always used it. Once, she got a bad fright. She'd headed far out, beyond the silt and sand of the shallows. It was almost imperceptible, the slightest jerk, but suddenly she turned, and the rhythm and grace had vanished from her stroke. She made for the shore, face tight, eyes wide with terror. "Wee Menlo'll catch you!" I shouted, teasing. I shouted it again and again until the lake rang with the distant, fairy-like echo of laughter. When she reached shore, gasping and trembling, I threw her a towel. "What happened, Cass?"

"Nothing," she muttered. "A rope perhaps." But she hardly spoke to me for a week.

I strolled across the lawn, hands in my pockets, and headed for the old yard. The lawn had been re-seeded, felt firm and dry underfoot, the grass spiky and prim like shaved armpits. I turned the corner of the conservatory to enter the yard, excited and pleased at this snatched moment in which I could enjoy my haven, alone. But the sense of foreboding which had begun to rise like purply thunderclouds when I spied the missing laurel hedge earlier, now came to a head. Such was the bubble of anxiety within, that my heart began to palpitate. The sheer possessiveness of it, I chided. Arianna McGregor. Let someone brush the nerve of the past, tamper in the slightest with the symbols of your creativity, and you're reduced to a caricature, a typical, introspective neurotic. Rational-isation failed. This encroachment was not slight, in any sense.

At the entrance to the yard, there now stood a fine pair of wrought-iron gates, tall, black and intimid-ating, yet somehow the most appropriate alteration

I'd met with. I couldn't see through them, they were too ornate, but the absolute delights of the past would be mine within seconds. Only later did it strike me that the creamy roses which used to arch carelessly each summer, had vanished. I pressed the lever and pushed.

The barn was gone. The place where I'd rest my canvas on a summer evening or occasionally sleep on a warm night. I was aware now of feeling like a child, met with an infantile, crushing sense of loss, the stultifying heart-scald of the irretrievable. There was no sign that it had ever, ever existed. In a half-shocked state, I treaded across a flat courtyard of terracotta tiling which was interrupted here and there by saplings. The centre-piece to this gesture of wanton philistinism was a hefty cherub mounted on a Corinthian column. I heard the sound of running water behind, turned and nearly stumbled into a fishpond. My stomach tensed. In an instant I had been reduced. The subject-matter, the source material of interviews, around which a recently acquired biographer was to make an investigative perusal, had been deleted. Worse, something seminal, which transcended self-esteem, had been excised, the residue scoured until it was a modern pleasantry, a contrivance, rootless and atemporal.

The orchard beyond the yard had been our retreat in time of domestic crime and youthful malfeasance. My lips tightened involuntarily into that expression which Cassandra and Manfred say makes me look like a thoroughly discontented woman (their euphemism for spinster) when the tides of our ménage run *contre moi*. There now stood three rows of young

127

trees, pristine and well-tended, which like most young and well-tended things would, doubtless, yield a decent crop. That was what bothered me. The yard had served no obvious purpose. Nor had the orchard. I could imagine Marie, Justin and the children sunning themselves *en famille* when the weather favoured such activities, on the right sort of sunbed in the right type of swimwear. Not naked and on blankets like we would have done. And the orchard harmless, beautiful in its lack of productivity, dazzlingly so because it was devoid of purpose, mossy and unpruned. The place was a rich weave, primed to make us intricate and difficult, to use us, have us continue a process of fulfilment, part of the gradual sheafing and absorption that made us want to write and paint.

Damn Marie, I thought. Damn her social aspirations and her longing from childhood to set foot in the house because she thought that we considered ourselves above her. Maybe we were. But in a way she'd never have understood. It had nothing to do with social equality or disparity. It went deeper, to parentage and experience and memory, an intellectual vitality on both sides. It had nothing to do with possession or money. It wasn't, I realised, as if they'd even stay there, grow as a family and let it wax in their experience until it was part of them. That was what irked most. My cheeks quivered. This was just a stepping-stone. To something bigger and better from which they would also pick the flesh, turn into a bastard, unloved version of themselves because they felt no pride in their past and must forever seek the cure to a voracious insecurity which might perhaps be half-assuaged when they had plonked themselves on an even higher hill.

"Are you day-dreaming again?"

I turned to find her behind me.

"You were always a bit of a dreamer," she giggled shyly. I said nothing. "Sorry about that delay," she rambled, "I'm involved in a bridge tournament and my partner is a real fanatic." I must have looked vacant, because she paused then, unsure of what she should say next.

"Yes," I said, trying to sound pleasant. "They say it's highly absorbing. I've no understanding of card games." Then I passed some innocuous remark about there being a lot of changes.

"I knew you wouldn't be disappointed," she said, looking at me with unusual directness, assuming approval in her childlike way.

"The Italian garden was a good idea, don't you find? Tidies things up somewhat." She stopped suddenly.

"Not that I meant..."

I raised my eyebrows, would not smooth the path for her this time.

"Yes?" I looked at her, wide-eyed.

"Well, you know..."

She was flustered now.

"Times change, don't they?" She smiled an olive-branch smile.

I watched from behind as she led the way back. People don't change much, in essence. You can still net the same expressions, recognise the aspirations and insecurities that wounded them as children. She chattered on, talking about the garden, then about having converted the old larder (Cassandra's workroom) into a study for Justin. I rolled my eyes behind her, remembering Justin as I'd known him. Despite my indignation, I suppressed a laugh.

"It was good of you to have me, dear." Defiant to the last that there should be no betrayals. She urged me to stay. But I couldn't bear any more. The feeling of slight abrasiveness I'd experienced when driving there, had grown to a state of fury and jealousy. The jealousy would be temporary, the fury unremitting. Because she had destroyed the jewel of our experience in a gesture of blithe thoughtlessness that was typical, perhaps her only inheritance.

"Give my regards to Cassandra...don't forget!" she shouted as I revved up. I unrolled the window.

"Maybe we'll all come next time!" I called, deliberately, delighted then at my mischief as she juggled mentally with sleeping arrangements and tried to conceal her surprise at the prospect of the three of us beneath the roof. I sent gravel and dust flying in clouds as I took the first corner of the avenue in third gear. I was glad. I wouldn't have liked her to have seen my face then, as I wondered what I was going to tell Cassandra.

Scavengers

Jack's house overlooks the seafront. On fogged winter evenings when rehearsals are in full swing, mother sometimes asks you to join her there, when you've done your homework. They are assembled casually, principals and perhaps a few of the chorus, the artistic soul of Clonfoy, once more rallying to the call of art while the sea spitefully lashes the harbour.

Nominally, it's a rehearsal. You know that by the time the quartet from *The White Horse Inn*, or the chorus from *The Maid of the Mountains* is sung, the serious business of the evening is over. In a sense. Jack, who usually has a cameo role of some sort, busies himself making tea, resplendent in a plum-coloured satin smoking-jacket, while the ladies slice Swiss rolls and sandwich-cakes.

You always go. Dorian is there. He pays scant attention to you but at least you can pass a few hours within the aura of The Presence. Jack's piano stands near the balcony windows and Dorian flexes his fingers importantly, while the leads cluster close, eyeing the score intently.

"That was a bit sharp—take the last four bars

again," Dorian might say, to Cassie usually. Her voice is high and forced, the shrill discordance needling its way to the eardrums. Dorian winces slightly as she zooms off-key again, or slurs indulgently down from high soh to doh. What commences with patience on his part, deteriorates gradually to a sizzling restraint, as Cassie continues to strike sharp from time to time.

"Can't break her from that habit," he says between his teeth to mother. "No ear, you see. She can't hear it in her head." You are dazzled. Even then, mother is half in love with him. He looks slightly ferocious, his fine dark hair hanging limply over a perspiring forehead.

"He's a true artist," she claims by way of explanation, when Dorian becomes irritable with the chorus.

"He suffers for it," she adds, shaking her head dolefully.

"Mm," you reply acquiescently, determined to sound neutral.

"Why does he behave so stupidly when he's drunk then?" you ask disapprovingly in the next breath, unconsciously ferreting your way into a wound and rubbing salt into it. You've heard stories about Dorian's demented binges. Saw him carried on a stretcher off the lifeboat, trembling dreadfully. After he'd gone out in someone's skiff and run it into The Ridge. You remember the smell. The stench of alcohol and vomit. And father.

Mother pauses, takes a sharp breath to steel herself against the ignorance of extreme youth. "He can't help it, Laura,"—she is nothing if not sympathetic—"he's driven to it. Things get to him."

You withdraw, wary of her insights.

One evening in early spring, she asks you to accompany her to Jack's, the fourth time in two weeks. You go anyway, enjoy watching the singers, listening to the tender humming and aahing as vocal chords are warmed up, primed amidst numerous arpeggios, the prelude to any musical rendering. You, of course, will never, ever, achieve their level of ease and gregariousness. Their music enthrals, despite Cassie of the dreaded F sharp. Count Danilo places his hands on Olga's waist and whirls her to his chest. You sit riveted. How can they *do* that without getting embarrassed, you ponder again. Mother sits on the piano-stool with Dorian. They play a duet. There is something rather sober-looking about them, compared to the others who by this stage have uncorked bottles of dark wine: love is as sombre as it is riotous, you discover. The music is like a twisting or stirring in your body, and perhaps somewhere else that doesn't have a name. It hurts, make you sense happiness. You know that you will cry into the bedroom curtains when you get home, try to stifle this strange, churning sensation.

Then he asks her to sing, and you sense that she is pleased. "Come on Toni," he coaxes, "try 'I'm a Stranger in Paradise'." Before she can protest the first chords fill the room. The others gradually stop talking. Mother stands behind Dorian, gazes out the window as she sings, her eyes looking along the damp, narrow road that skirts the harbour, beyond the sulphurous yellow glow from the street lights. Everybody listens. She sways to the rhythm of the song. Their faces gradually cloud to seriousness. Then at the end, they clap and yahoo, and her eyes are bright, her smile nervous.

It is your last year, the final lap of an insufferable ordeal at the hands of fact-saturating bores. But on your treks to and from school, there is the possibility of meeting Dorian in his frosted blue Scirrocco. He always sees you, waves casually or winks. You are convinced that he finds you attractive, ever since the evening at Jack's place when he remarked to someone that you had "a nice little figure". You are hungry for praise. Even these meagre crumbs satisfy. You learn what it is to scavenge, to gnaw on pickings, nibble on bones. Without any doubt, you know that mother has beaten you to it. The main kill. Without even trying. Dorian is hers, for no other reason except alignment of age, experience and attitude. She simply is.

So you bask in reflected light, something generated by others, pale as a winter sun by the time it reaches you. Sense conspiracies, yearn to be part of them. By comparison, school friendships are a web of crude emotions, as clumsy as large rusted nails driven crookedly into a frame, splintering the wood. The day is a prohibitive sequence of bells and instructions, well-meant advice and reprimands.

"If your poor father could see you now..."

"It still affects her, you know..."

"The mother exercises no control..."

Words, words, filter through to your consciousness. They offend. Yet your dreams stay intact. Other words like "bohemian" "cosmopolitan" and "experienced" rise from the bed of your mind, move like a slow tide around your waking thoughts, dispel the fear of stumbling feet and the coarse tongue that went with it. They kept you both silent. After the funeral, you cried with relief. A sweet, flushing relief.

You arrive home one day to find your mother and Dorian in the sitting-room. They have been laughing. You hear their voices as you open the back door, follow the sound, surprised to have visitors. Normally she rests or applies face-packs and eye-balms. "Ah, you're here, Laura!"—a little over-enthusiastic. They sit smiling at you, cups empty, crumbs on the coffee-table. You brace yourself. She gets straight to the point.

"Laura…" Hesitantly, fingers joined for a moment, as if unsure of what to say. Much like the way she joins her fingers before she sings. Preparing. Focusing her thoughts on something important.

"Dorian and I are thinking of taking a holiday soon. Maybe around Hallowe'en, we thought."

We thought. Dorian and I. Mother you're even sillier than I thought, and you know how he drinks, you know, you know.

"Yeah?" you grunt by way of a reply, attempting the road of neutrality, trying to strike an appropriate pose, to arrange your face in an expression of mild surprise and a less-than-tepid interest.

"Good idea!" you add then, more jauntily.

"Where d'you think you'll go?" you continue, feigning concessionary interest, determined to control yourself, to quiet the resentment that steams your mind with its heat.

"Well, we thought maybe London…"

Great. Just great. A furtive weekend in the metropolis. You force your face into a congratulatory,

137

approving smile.

"Sounds great to me anyway," and you shrug your shoulders.

Their relief is instant. It flows osmotically through the room from their bodies. You stroll out again, head for the piano in the other room. You cannot muster the energy to attempt the "Polonaise," the "Marche Militaire," or "Zug der Zwerge". You tinkle apathetically for some time, fingers on automatic control, while your mind rages within its confines. You cannot cry. Not yet, not yet. Crying belongs to the night, in the oceanic quiet of dark, the secret peace, when the beast moves out, far out across the rocks, into the heaving breast of the sea, to thresh in its lonely turmoil.

You have lost the morsels of Dorian's attention that used to fall down your open gullet. His glances. A chance touch against your arm. Things mother seems not to notice, or if she does, not to care about. That afternoon, he stays to tea, and afterwards they drive to Jack's, for one final rehearsal of *The Gondoliers*. A family again. Whole and complete. Wheee! They sing even as they leave—"Dance a Cachuca, Fandango, Bolero." Your face feels unbearably heavy as you hear their jokes and remarks. How childish they are.

You can't prevent yourself thinking about them, about what they are going to do in London. It does not dawn on you that they have probably done it already. You have a highly developed sense of protocol, and London, or somewhere labelled "away", is the appropriate location for the consummation of such matters. You retire early, shored-up. A grotesque untouchable whose needs are of such abnormal proportions that none must ever guess at the quivering beast that lies seconds behind your smooth face.

All through the musical "season" you simmer, smart inwardly each time you examine her bright face, focused on Dorian's equally radiant one. The house is filled with music. You cannot wake in the mornings without hearing mother's voice as she practises scales after the ritual drink of hot honey and lemon. To soothe the vocal chords. You tire of the "Cachuca, Fandango, Bolero," and "The Duke of Plaza-Toro," the vigorous renderings of which now seem incessant and a necessary component of life at home.

There is no escape. You pass the concert-hall one evening just as the chorus is belting out the finale. The audience is clapping in time to the music. This makes it for the singers, if not for Dorian, who never admits to being pleased about any show, by way of implying how impossibly high his standards are. In an instant, you see what it all means. Camaraderie and rivalry. What it means to recognise that Cassie is singing sharp once again. What it means to dance in a dress with a velvet bodice that pinches your waist. What it is to hear applause because the audience likes your music, likes what you love, what is inextricably part of you because it forces you to feel things. We push at the horizon, all of us. At any minute, we could be being born, might break the skin that separates us from ourselves, but it is a hungry struggle, a dark, vital, passion-ridden business that begs to be satisfied. So much of it is hunger.

The next morning you expect mother to be buoyant.

Instead, she sits rather despondently at breakfast, as you rush around, late as usual. Her dressing-gown hangs half-open, and for the first time since father's death she is smoking.

"Cigarettes?" you half-squeak.

She glances up. You might be a crustacean that has wandered in from the shore during the night.

"Ah..." she sighs, runs her hand back through her hair. Traces of Leichner make-up have yellowed the roots at the front.

"I just felt like one, and the show's over anyway."

"But your voice, mother..." you begin hastily.

She interrupts swiftly, will not suffer fools at this early hour. "Won't do me any harm—this once," and she smiles by way of silencing you. A patronising smile, reserved only for the young or the infirm. You pull the door sharply. Quite clearly, she thinks you know nothing. Understand nothing. You long for revenge of some sort, sit nettled all day, absorbed in the plot of *Retribution*, a drama in three parts which will take place at some indeterminate juncture of your future.

Nevertheless, when she invites you to accompany her to Jack's for one last round of songs before the society breaks up for a few months, you cannot resist. Their world still beckons, subtly and forcefully, seduces like a wholesome meal. Oddly enough, Dorian is absent. Jack mumbles something to mother, who looks disconcerted. You scrutinise her face. It betrays little, but when she speaks, you notice that her voice has lost its smoothness, presents a rasping quality which hitherto had not been there. She's been smoking all day. Someone plays the piano, leads into a set of numbers from past shows—*Showboat*, *Porgy and Bess*, *Kismet*. Soon the room is warm, throbs with the sound of sopranos, altos, baritones, Jeanette MacDonalds and Count John McCormacks. They sway together, look pleased and serious, wrapped in their own virtuosity.

Just as they prepare to launch into the second verse of "Good-bye" where bold Leopold marches off for the sake of the fatherland, a car skids wildly to a halt somewhere beyond the house. To my surprise, everyone grows silent. Mother looks anxious. She is flushed. Twists her fingers uneasily, runs her rings up and over the knuckles. The fellow at the piano attempts to stoke things up again, but the moment has passed. The doorbell rings. "Who the hell can that be?" Jack, muttering, glances quickly at her. There's a lot of noise in the hall then, the sound of heavy footsteps, the door slamming loudly. Above it all, Dorian's voice, garrulous.

He stumbles in. Suddenly the men are around him, saying things like "You're all right, you're all right," and "Take it easy now." But he doesn't. You shrink at the tirade, words vile and insulting. You don't understand everything. His mouth is twisted and ugly, flaps uselessly, like a torn pocket. Then he turns on mother. Moves towards her. She stands up.

"Toni," he begins, leaning against her, talking into her face. You can smell his breath from where you sit. Reel with a nauseous sense of nightmare. Nightmare. Night-mare. *Mare:* sea. Neuter noun. Third declension. That steely darkness whence the beast comes at dawn, returns at night. How often he did that. Came and went. Came and went, like a violent tide, battering you both into submission. Over and over.

His eyes, red-rimmed and watery, peer into her face. Saliva trembles on his lower lip. You want to close your eyes.

"Not now, Dorian," she says gently, trying to push him from her. Her gentleness is beyond you.

"Now now," he repeats thickly, while the others whisper, or try to pretend that nothing untoward is occurring.

"Not now?" he repeats, his voice rising in a drunken question. He pauses, calling on the remnants of his consciousness, sways slightly. "Well *when*?" he roars, his fingers gripping the top of her arm. Sweat rolls on your back and your eyes prickle with the threat of tears.

Suddenly her expression is one of helplessness. He launches into an incoherent stream of language which strikes your ears like grapeshot. He shouts, makes ugly sounds with ugly words. You remember the words "merry" and "widow," his mocking tone, his fist coming down on the piano keyboard as he chants a few bars of the waltz. Jack tries to intervene with pleas of "That's enough now, that's enough," and someone else keeps repeating "You're all right, you're all right," while he tears at her flesh, strips her of music, of love, spits all in her face. He actually spits at her. Somebody starts to pat your shoulder then. You roar back that it isn't all right, your face crumpling in on itself as the sobbing begins. As something hateful and familiar begins to circle your brain, treading, treading, a tormented hunger, pacing, pacing, locked within itself, focused on the sight of father's face, ridiculously peaceful after the accident.

Yet this time, you cry for her. All the way home, she drives with her face set rigidly, while you sniffle in the passenger seat. You have not anticipated such a dénouement, such humiliation, have misinterpreted the signs and the skies. It is so undignified. So devoid of all that you cherish. There is baseness everywhere. For the first time in your life, you pity your mother, want so to recreate the world that she might be spared Dorian, his demonic binges. That she, that you both, might know what is real, might reject the wild spawn of a charlatan muse.

As you get out of the car, you blow your nose. She locks up, walks ahead to the front door. Stops then, and turns to you, her eyes large and tired. A foghorn blows, long and sonorous, and grey mist smothers the windows and roofs of every house. How ghostly she is then. You shut the door on the town, in an effort to seal off the talk which, inevitably, will break like a flood-tide the next day, frothy with inaccuracies and frequent re-telling. Stuff that will be sniffed at, picked over behind safe walls, till the bones are well-exposed.

The Adulteress

T he year I knew Rainer was a lonely one. It was cold and harsh, and it seemed as if I did everything alone. We were married one year at that time and we were poor, not at starvation level but greatly restricted financially, so that our life then contrasted cruelly with the life we had led before marriage. He was working to repay our various loans, while I was engaged in a post-graduate course of study.

Our house was to me at that time dull, anonymous, matching our lives perfectly in that respect. I was twenty-four and had been underemployed for the past year as a library assistant, found my wages eaten into by income tax by more than a third and had convinced myself that there had to be more to life. Believing that I could grasp my own destiny and form it at will, I returned to the university, my hopes of escape from the anonymity of my existence high, my vanity soaring at the challenge of doing an MA. I was determined to realise myself intellectually, because my self-esteem had plummeted during the past year, with the difficult adjustments of marriage and the hair-splitting of my co-workers in the library.

The moment I saw Rainer I was secretly delighted

and immediately felt guilty that I—hardly a year wed—could be so excited by this tall German from Bayreuth. I was also quite amused by him, by his obvious vanity and contrived bohemianism—the carefully tousled blonde hair contrasting with the neatly trimmed beard and moustache, the silk cravat on his white throat and the endless cigarettes. Everything about him spoke of "the artist" in the stereotypical sense of the word, and for a long time I was inclined not to take him seriously, even though he was to be one of my teachers for the year.

It all began in small ways. From the moment I left the house and cycled up through the estate I was on my way to another world, a world which I, gifted, recognised, and financially secure, would eventually occupy. My mind always raced ahead as I cycled down the narrow road towards the village, eyes running in the icy atmosphere, avoiding potholes and patches of ice as I mounted the canal bridge. Occasionally I'd halt on the bridge, to watch a train pass beneath, or to observe the swans that paddled the greeny canal, tearing at plankton every so often but keeping a watchful eye on passers-by. Looking down the hill from the bridge, the village seemed to me shrouded in frost-mists, distant, almost mediaeval, humped in upon itself, its lowness broken only by the church spire and the Gothic austerity of the college. I relished the churning sound of the mill and the odour of grain ripening the air at that early hour. From that standpoint, I could imagine a different place entirely, a crusty, cobbled, yellow-stoned village in a Bertolucci film, with swarthy peasants, rattling carts, squealing pigs and the sonorous knelling from the church lending the atmosphere of another time. But that too was my stereotypical perception of a medieval village.

In any case, Maynooth I decided, as I cycled down the main street, avoiding potholes, taking the corner for the Galway Road in style, could be nothing else but Maynooth—grubby and mean, part of the low-lying, windswept, black, unforgiving world that made up the midlands. As I pedalled on towards the new campus I would begin to think about Rainer, how he might look that day, how I would act, because I knew I must always prepare myself for the turmoil that took place within me three times a week. I admitted to myself quickly that I liked him, that I was drawn to him strongly, but I knew I must never betray myself. Apart from that, I felt a little guilty. I could not believe that I could feel like this so soon. This was the type of thing I associated with the "seven-year-itch" syndrome. But I was quite bored with our lives, with the seeming lack of direction, so perhaps it was natural that Rainer, blonde, exotic, tantalising Rainer, should make me quake again with that delicious vitality which comes from being desired—and desiring.

He never knew how much he tortured me, what I suffered in his presence, how I grew to want him. My lectures with him usually lasted two hours. He was intensely interested in his subject, Medieval Studies, and so, as it happened, was I. One of the central concepts in mediaeval German literature was "Minne" or "love," so much of the year was devoted to a close study of what is known as *Deutscher Minnesang*. Ironic, to say the least. It was natural therefore, that when we took a break half-way through a session, which was really a discussion, not a lecture proper, as I was the only student, that the conversation continued. Over cups of coffee and Cheshire cake we mulled over the inequities of love, the ill-aligned relationships, the short-lived, intense sputterings of erotic love, and what Rainer saw then as the decidedly duller norms of the long-term relationship. In a way we were talking about ourselves, something which was certainly of heightened interest to both of us. All the time I longed to reach out my hand and say, "I'm that person: I'm the one you could have it all with," ached to touch him, to kiss him. But I had to be patient, had to play that foul game of seeming detachment, that fall from human dignity which marks modern society: I had to play cool, had to conduct myself as if he were just anybody, as if everything we discussed was being considered purely objectively, when all along it consumed me.

Listening to him back in his study, I liked to look at his eyes. We could always meet one another's eyes. There was no shy flickering downwards, no aversion of the head. Looking at his eyes I would wonder if he was searching within mine for some sign, something to indicate a mutual passion. It was practically the only way I ever dared face him, through my own eyes. I would look greedily into his, enjoying the fact that he always met my gaze and held it as he talked, elevating the day from the blue frostiness of Maynooth to something indescribably warm, intimate.

In Walther von der Vogelweide's poem *"Traumliebe"* [A Dream of Love], he would ponder excessively on the various meanings of the word "kranz", as in "Nemt, frouwe, disen kranz!" Not only was it a wreath, but its circularity was a symbol of the hymen, what the medievals saw as a flowery fortress which in courtly love, could only be transgressed through marriage. Yes, perhaps he dwelt a little too long on lines like:

> wizer unde roter bluomen weiz ich vil:
> die stent niht verre in jener heide.
> da si schone entspringent
> und die vogele singent,
> da suln wir si brechen beide

> [I know of many white and red flowers:
> They lie not far beyond that meadow.
> We two shall pluck them, there,
> where they spring so beautifully
> and where the birds sing...]

Doubtless, we both contained within us a dream of love, an unexplained, unfulfilled dream of erotic love. But we never spoke of it directly, made no attempt to move one towards the other. He was kind in that respect. He did not set out to play games, to torture me by teasing. But at the same time, we could have studied other things, could have given our energies to the translation of *Gregorious*. Instead, there was the whole of *Deutscher Minnesang*, selected tracts of *Des Minnesangs Frühling* and an extensive study of the *Carmina Burana*.

One day he came to my home. It was to arrange my lecture schedule for the following term: as usual, something innocuous, harmless, which could have been done by telephone. He entered the house slowly, looking around constantly, the blue eyes shifting here and there as he took in the furnishings, the pictures, the shades and nuances of my life with my husband. We drank coffee and listened to a tape. As the music blasted from the speakers (*O Fortuna, velut lunae*) I was uplifted, filled with him, had to acknowledge now that we were alone in the large peach-walled room insulated from the world by the frenetic outpourings of the *Carmina Burana*, that we would have been well suited, in every way. As soon as I said it to myself, as soon as I faced the truth, there came a sense of loss, sorrow, frustration that there was nothing to be done, nothing I dared do. Because I had nothing to hinge my feelings upon. He had given no signal and neither had I. We simply looked at each other that afternoon, from opposite sides of the room, circling one another's souls, probing, making love in the silent place in the head, where there were no conventions, no truces, no treaties, no imperatives, but a collective loving union which was without the anchor of possession and jealousy, the anchor of monogamy.

According to the bible, I am an adulteress. Simply by desiring another man I have, according to the bible, committed adultery. If that is so then we are all doomed by our intense yearnings, by those dreams which awaken us in the night with a full throat and leave us lying fitfully through the grey dawn when something mundane like the alarm-clock going off, or the need to go to the bathroom, brings us back to our senses. No, *senses* is hardly the right word. We are brought back to the callousness of everyday imperatives: the necessity of keeping the show going, of keeping on humanity's trek towards who-knows-what, some warped and vague morality, some thunderous God-in-the-skies who keeps the stars spinning through eternal blackness for their sin of being bright. That is what we are brought back to with the dawn. The senses are another thing.

When I was with him, whether alone or with others, my senses took over, brought into operation a finely-tuned system of perception which ensured that I missed not even his slightest move, absorbed in his smile, his voice with its rough Bavarian texture. And all the time I was acting, revolting myself by playing cool because I had to, while at heart I was confused and anxious . No one would have guessed. In the first place those who knew me also knew that I had married only the previous year, and naturally assumed with all their nudge-winkery that my eyes remained monogamously in one place. In our society, it was time for them to be looking surreptitiously for bumps, for signs of thickening on my body, even though I was already committed to another course of activity.

We are all polygamous, and none more so than women. I know that I keep a rein on myself voluntarily because in general, the life I lead, which is a strictly monogamous one, has a preciousness which I would not now forsake, could not. We have shared much together and we have grown to love one another in a real sense. But at that time, I could easily have faltered. I was not so sure of myself, or of life. Like a child let loose in a well-stocked pantry I was impatient to sample the goodies on the heavily-laden shelves, and devour the first colourful and sweet thing I touched, whilst eyeing everything else greedily. Though I wanted, I could not have, Rainer. I had chosen. Nonetheless, polygamy runs deep in us all. It has occasionally been speculated that women were originally polygamous, and that the trappings of western morality which characterise the main churches, are rigorously designed to ensure that they will stay monogamous. It sounds a faulty piece of speculation to me. Child-rearing has always tended to attach a woman to one particular hunter/bread-winner, despite her erotic instincts.

But there are certain days even still, when I am full of love for every man I meet. Not in any obvious way. It's more an upsurge of feeling within me which causes me to wish I could make love to the lot of them, take my pick: "I'll have you, and you—no, not you—you there in the dusty denims—you, you and you," as if it were the most natural thing in the world for a woman to take her pick. And what a hypocrite I feel at times, striding about like any Mrs Normal, greeting this one and that one, buying meat, going to work, being generally civil to all and sundry. How boring that can be.

As the year drew to a close, I became slightly more daring, was resolved that Rainer should not go from my life without some good memory. The first day of May that year we met in Bewley's in Grafton Street, for a tutorial because the college had not yet re-opened after Easter recess. I had looked forward to it all week and arrived at the restaurant in a state of some inner excitement. That was the first signal. I recognised it so easily because I had noticed it in others before. I had seen it between Alma, a friend from my undergraduate days, and a theology student, when they were still secretive about their relationship, had noticed instantly one day in the college canteen, how their legs touched, knee to knee under the table, and how neither of them shifted position as one would normally do. The same thing happened here. Rainer rattled on about Heinrich von Morungen, having ordered coffee and cakes, and somehow, his leg touched mine. It was a gentle pressure, warm, secret, intimate, and I did not move. I dropped my hand to my lap, and as I did so, he grasped it quickly, clasped it gently, talking all the time about von Morungen's differentiated *Kunstform*. I returned the slight pressure and our tutorial continued amidst the clatter of cups and knives, the warm odour of the restaurant, amidst the clusters of young people in light T-shirts or pantaloons, for it was—truly—the first day of summer, a day of golden translucence which deemed the reefing ice-age of Maynooth dead.

That was all. No word was spoken. There were no declarations of love, or desire, no obvious concessions to our mood beyond the open glance which we had always shared. In that moment when he took my hand I was partly released from myself, from the convoluted frustrations of the year, the solitariness of my study, the aloneness of the campus (because all my friends had left by this stage, to teach or plot their respective paths in the world), the unending battle within. By taking my hand, by that gentle pressure on my leg, he had said what I wanted to hear. I felt somewhat lighter, relieved, as we walked along Grafton Street. Coming behind me in the crowds that jostled at every turn, he remarked in his halting way that my hair was a nice colour, and touched it, scarcely touched it with his hand.

It was then a shower broke, sent the sun-happy hordes scattering for shelter. We continued our walk towards Trinity, moving slowly along Nassau Street together, he holding an umbrella above both of us. For those few yards, until we entered the Lecky, I permitted myself to wonder, indulged my fancies and desires, tried to imagine what it would be like if it were always like this. Would I turn towards another after a time? Of course I felt I would not, that this was the ultimate and that I was denying myself nobly at every turn for the sake of "the marriage".

As we walked into Trinity, it felt so natural to be with Rainer but then it always feels "natural" does it not, when we are with those whose company we languish for?

That was our only transgression, if you could call it that. Afterwards there remained only the end-of-term party, organised by the German Department, usually a tacky affair in an over-large under-heated room. But somebody had made it look inviting, for when we entered, my husband and I, we were struck by the warm ambience, the pink aura created by wrapping papier-mâché around the lampshades, the odour of *Glühwein* spicing the air warmly. Rainer was there, and ladled it out for us, smiling, obviously merry. "*Guten Rutsch ins neue Jahr!*" he drawled at us, raising his glass to the new year. "*Hör mal—jetzt ist Sommer Rainer, jetzt is Sommer!*" "But it's summer, it's summer now," I insisted soberly. "*Na dann, 'st Winter, Winter auf immer...*" he muttered and moved to the piano, placing his glass on the open top. What followed was about fifteen minutes of mad, crazy, professionally-played jazz, and while he jangled, spangled our dreams, we danced. Everybody joined in the general frivolity, Rainer watching us, smiling, his small even teeth visible as he played and smiled, smiled and played.

That night, although I hated myself for it afterwards, I made love to my husband imagining all the while that he was Rainer. Now I could give in to it, finally, could indulge the feelings which I'd kept at bay all year. For it no longer mattered. Rainer would return to Germany. I would take my examination, and depending on the result, would either seek immediate employment or head for further glories. Besides, the strain of it all was tiring. I needed a break.

Summer passed slowly. I studied in the library each day, tramping down through the village, or drove, passing through the tall wrought-iron gates, past the dozing security-man, into the old campus, enjoying the pungency of the summer flowers and shrubs, the air filled with the frenetic humming of bees and the call of pigeons as they flew heavily across the square. Nearly every day I met the same few priests as they enjoyed a post-prandial stroll along the same strip of the square, moving down past the magnolia, the willow, the weeping eucalyptus, the rose-beds, stopping at the pampas-grasses, doing an about-turn and proceeding back in the direction from where they had come. But my mind was elsewhere. Not exactly on Rainer. My peace of mind had utterly dissolved, abnegated in the fret and fever of study, so that I was no longer rising to a challenge as had been the case originally but was biding my time until the exam was done with, until I had my MA and could be free of the damned place for good.

For the first time in my life I failed an examination. My hand would scarcely grip the telephone receiver properly as they told me I'd failed, and I dropped it gingerly back on its cradle, rooted to the spot, seeing my future, my passport to the status I craved, shatter cruelly like any piece of fragile porcelain at my feet. There were other factors involved besides Rainer. I did not fail because of him. He was only a part, a component in the situation.

I will never forget how awful it was to fail. For a week I spoke to nobody on the telephone, locked myself away in the bedroom and gratefully accepted my husband's ministrations, the cups of tea, the cigarettes, the trinkets he bought in order to humour me, to tease me back to a state of normality. Eventually I rose to his baits. This was rock bottom, I thought. The only direction had to be up. It was as simple as that. Within three months I had more or less recovered a semblance of normality—at least I was not depressed. Instead I was bitter. Most of all, this bitterness was directed in part at Rainer, though I knew he was not responsible in any way for my failure; that had been my own fault. He wrote me a letter, sympathising with my misfortune, and enclosed a photograph of himself. That was the ultimate, the final insulting act of vanity. I tore it to shreds. Yes, I was angry that he had ever existed within the confines of my life, that he had appeared as it were, to prod me along the path towards academic and (temporary) emotional disaster. But there is no diceman, no prodigious finger which pushes you haphazardly from point to point. Any decisions taken were mine. My mistake, if that it be, was that I was—am—a romantic, an ill-fitting joist in the clean pragmatism of the times. I fell foul of that tendency (which absorbs many adolescents for hours) to daydream. It has to be said. That was how I compensated for what I saw as a frustrating and mundane existence.

The saddest, most bitter moment for me came when, grim-faced and filled with trepidation, I sat on the bus on a wet November morning, heading into one of the Dublin hospitals to begin a secretarial job, that non-career in which the unambitious can pass their years. There was nothing, as far as I was concerned, to look forward to. Sitting towards the back of the bus which was stopped in the traffic which jammed Chapelizod Bridge, I gazed idly from the window, half-hypnotised into a self-deceiving state of torpor which I thought was calmness. Then I saw him. Just as he spotted me. Rainer had come back. He waved up from the small red car which he drove, smiling. It was too much. I ignored his wave and looked away.

Honey Island

t's not so much the Earl Grey tea and the sudden knowledge of wines. Nor indeed the thoughts of what they did together when he was away. But the chance discovery at the post-office on the other side of the island. Does he not know that she cycles there to stock up on peppermints, the creamy thick soft ones which old Mr Fuller brings in from the mainland, that she then sells at the crafts shop?

Three artists rent the two rooms behind the shop for a pittance every summer. Pleasant, downy-faced young Americans intent on bringing light and joy to the world through their art. This year there's an oil painter, his colours carnival reds, garrulous yellows and threatening blacks. He is more manic than the usual type, reminding her of the Czech who once stayed. His wife works on leather, cuts belts and amulets, textured brown pouches which sell more easily than the painter's work. With them is a potter, a middle-aged man. She does not understand the relationship between the three, but knows she could have *him*, recognises the hopeful tindering in his eyes when he looks at her, which she never reciprocates.

What tears still is the loss of innocence. She

remembers growing up there, the frantic, happy hours of waiting for the Christmas trawler, of wondering would the tides favour them. In the summers, the thrill of ice-cream. Her father rows to the mainland on Sunday mornings, buys a couple of packs of creamy ripple and ten choc-ices, wraps them in sheets of newspaper and rows like the devil back to the island before the stuff melts. On the pier, she waits, the fleet-footed one, legs longer than her brothers, grabs the package and shins up the beach and across the dunes to their house.

Her long legs and the need for exercise is what keeps her cycling. Summer visitors come to know her as she pumps along. She never tires of the twenty-mile stretch of land called Ilnameala, *Oilean Na Meala*, or Honey Island, so called because of a monastic settlement in the ninth century and the work of one, bee-keeping monk. It is said that the beeswax from Ilnameala could be sculpted to a hard perfection unheard of before, that chalices, goblets, even tabernacles could be formed from the stuff.

This is what Aengus teaches the children in the small primary school, and whether it is true or not, she agrees with him. The children must know such things. Despite his godlessness he has fitted into island life with ease. The ten years have been tough, sinewy times, but also satisfying. There are few words to describe what she feels. But he has always been different. For one thing he comes from the mainland and for another he's a man always in a state of wanting what he cannot have.

Their table sits at the west window. They are at tea, he skimming his bread lightly with butter, she laying it on in thick shiny welts. Their favourite view is from this side of the house, facing the bay where cloud-shadows make mosaics of colour on the water. To the left of the window is the photograph taken by some local chap late in the afternoon when Aengus and she rowed in for good ten years ago, after the honeymoon. It is underexposed, by accident rather than design, and they cut it from the local *Gazette*, recognising the tilt of Aengus's cap and the fuzz of her hair in what was intended to be a scenic photo. It is the mark of their beginning. Like a dream, the oars dip gently into the water, the mainland mountains fall behind their boat and light streams from behind clouds. She loves it because it is about them.

The honeymoon is a dull memory in comparison to the present. They eat contentedly this evening. It is the first food she has swallowed in two days. Her mouth is slightly swollen from kissing, his eyes gaze at her as if she were a wonder, the lashes drooping sleepily. It is a battle of sorts. They have asked the artists not to come for a while.

"We understand," the painter says soulfully.

"Everybody needs time alone," says his wife in her soft upstate New York accent.

Both Aengus and Hanna like the educated Americans. They are tolerant and optimistic, infinitely more bearable than the terrier second-generation Irish-Americans who occasionally visit Ilnameala only to go away disappointed because the monks left no decent ruins.

A couple of times a day for the past week, since her discovery, they try to forgive, to repossess. It has never been so exciting, they can hardly contain themselves after the talking and arguing is over, the sight of him leaving her weeping with desire, his mouth kindled again with wanting, soft and wide and wet. But it is a battle, and they know it. She has almost lost him—her mate, her man—to the woman in the mainland town.

"You didn't have to stay over with her," she accuses.

"I…wanted to," he replies doggedly, "…and I don't regret anything."

She lifts her knife and slices it through the air across the room. It lands in the empty fireplace.

"You bastard! You rotten bastard!" she says quietly, thoughts of him and the woman awakening the hurt and fury again.

"You stopped loving me," she says simply.

"Perhaps. I was convinced you didn't care any more," he says calmly.

"It suited you to think that," she spits.

She retrieves the knife and carries on eating, knows too well that she has to woo him back, believing that in spite of the lapse he cares. The love-making is proof, the way he groans "Oh Hanna, it's you, it's you I want, always wanted!", everything in him attending to her, stroking, eager for her. Still, she has to goad him to find out more. "You've taken me for granted too," she says, not looking at him, apparently concentrating on the evening boat as it disgorges more visitors down at the pier.

"Never."

"Yes. There are things I've never told you because I thought you'd leave."

She tells him then and his eyes widen in disbelief. The summer the Czech had rented the workshop. Vaclav and his wife. Right under his nose and he hadn't twigged what was happening. Angered by his trust she'd let it go on, in love with the man from the east yet not wanting to be. He was all talk, rhetoric, and she fell for it, flattered by good conversation and nice words, the flattery mutual as he sensed her interest in the miniature sculptures, sensuous figures made from epoxy resin, plaster and bronze. One of them he modelled on her shapely rump.

"You've got a great, beautiful backside," he said thickly.

His wife noticed nothing. It served them both right she thought then and still thinks. His wife and her husband. For taking things for granted, for assuming ownership when there can be no such thing, for being lazy lovers.

"O my God, O my God," he says over and over, hands covering his face as she lets it out, what has been dammed up in her these past five years.

"So you're not the only one. And you didn't know a thing about it. And I hated you for that," she tells him, raging, full of spite, wanting to punish.

"O how could you, how could you?" he asked, spinning away from the table, his body bent double as he sobs.

Just as quickly her rage evaporates and she is flooded with regret. She wants to put her arms around him but dare not. He is white with shock. She thinks she has surely lost him now, that he'll take the next boat and head off to the mainland to that woman who also loves him and with whom he claims to be in love. The obvious questions spill from him. How many others? How can he ever believe in her again?

"How can I ever believe in you?" she counters. Trust is one thing, but blind trust is folly where men and women are concerned. Something she has always believed, knowing herself to be attracted to the volatile, to the briefly dancing mote of light. But he has seen her as an islander, sturdily rooted to her craft-shop and generations of harsh survival, a woman making the odd foray to the mainland to stock up on books and expensive Alpaca wools from South America. The wools are her indulgence. A life of watching local weavers and knitters leaves no taste for the earthy salt-and-pepper tones of the local product, the sensible shoulder-lines, the stocking-stitch cuffs and turtle-necks. Those she leaves to Aengus, the outsider, the man for whom island living is still novel and utopian. For herself she knits rich purple tops with softly-draped, falling shoulder-lines, or mixes red yarn with purple and green, fixes the finished garment with diamanté buttons, or rough wooden clasps hewn in the workshop. Always, always, she wants seduction, wants the hand of the loved one to finger those buttons hopefully, expectantly, with the barest restraint. And if the loved one, the focus of attention, altered for a few weeks one summer, what of it, she tells him now.

"You were blind to it, you bloody fool!"

Vaclav knew how to undo those buttons, had teased back the garment just enough.

"This is terrible, I can't believe it..." he weeps now, shoulders heaving. She wants to hold him, but she is afraid, talks on instead, attempts to explain.

"There's one difference between me and you," she says finally. "I feel guilty about it."

The day at the post-office on the other side of the island is the worst moment. Just when she dares to hope, the wind at her back as she peddles energetically up the hill, bursting in on Mr Fuller for the usual chat and the few pounds of peppermints that are so popular on her side of the island. In retrospect she realises that he is unsure about something. An uncomfortable uncertainty lurks behind his conversation about the weather, the prospects of visitors as late as October, news of another oil-spill a couple of hundred miles northwards.

"Yes. Yes." He is hesitant.

"Well then, that's it. See you next week," she says cheerily, making to go.

"This came," he says simply, taking it from beneath the counter, confusion in his rheumy eyes.

She grabs it and runs for the bike, letting the peppermints fly where they will as the bag drops from her hand.

She stumbles into the house. He is preparing a large hotpot for the artists, who are to eat with them that day. The rock is raised high in her hand, as if she is drunk. But she is sober, mad with the hurt of it, mad at the contrivances and trouble he has taken to speak intimately to that woman. It isn't his head she's after, but the photograph. The rock crashes through the glass, which flies in all directions, cutting her hand. She rips the picture from the wall, slams it repeatedly against the table.

"Bastard, bastard, betraying swine, you bastard..."
Finally she tears what remains of the picture from the

split frame.

"Here," she tosses it towards him bitterly. "Jesus you didn't have to do that, you didn't have to let her write to Fuller's place, you could have had them sent here," she cries.

The madness tears at her again and she lifts a kitchen stool and starts to smash it against the walls.

"I want away, I want away. Let me go, I've got to get out—out!" she insists. Suddenly she feels him grabbing her: he has her by the belt of her trousers, pulling her towards him as she wrestles with the stool; she hears him say she never listened, that she didn't take him seriously, was never there when it counted, sure wasn't he mad about her, didn't he always love her, he couldn't let her go. Still she resists, fighting him all the way, struggling for the front door, staggering around him as he tries to pull her in.

"I hate you—I hate you—I love you, I never stopped loving you!" she screams, roaring incoherently between hate and love, over and over, wanting to scream till she dies. He is crying now, as the struggle ebbs, as he draws her in, as she lets him.

Their phone is in the crafts shop. They ask the artists if they'd mind going into the house while he uses it. The three nod compliantly, tolerance radiating again from their expressions. They like Aengus and Hanna. They've heard it all, the entire rumpus. Hasn't half the island. She waits outside in the garden, licks the blood off her hand, takes up a spade to poke at the weeds while he phones the mainland.

Trembling still, she listens to sounds that drift from the house. The artists help themselves; they fit in easily and tidily, enjoy the meals and conversations a few evenings each week.

Once, she glances over at the shop, glimpses him through a side-window, his handkerchief balled in one hand as he talks. He has taken the decision himself. That means they have a chance. She can still woo him out of it. There is no anger for the other woman now, nor for him, though it will come and go between them, like tides beyond their control. She will write once to the woman who has loved him so well. She must talk to her, tell her things.

After it, they leave the artists to their meal and their wine. Her jumper is in tatters, where a splinter from the stool caught on the wool. The smell of food fills the house, wafts into the bedroom. Words are uttered over and over, sounds of comfort. There are mad, eager movements as they discover what they never knew before.

The Other Country

Andy's face froze as he took in the scene. Madeline grabbed the child and examined what remained of the thumb. Zoë roared. Blood pumped furiously from the severed joint, darkening her shorts, ran in delta-like rivulets down her legs and into yellow sandals.

"Get a doctor for Christ's sake!" Madeline called icily, absorbed by the child's horror, ripping the sleeve from her own blouse in the urgency of making a tourniquet. Freda, the neighbour whose son had unwittingly snapped hedge-clippers across Zoë's thumb, tried to calm her offspring. He roared in tandem with Zoë, appalled at the monstrosity of the unintended crime, gulping hysterically from time to time.

"It's all right Jimmy," Freda said, red-faced. "It's all right, all right." It was a chant which half-registered with Madeline, almost calming her too. Difficult to be calm when Zoë was screaming her head off. Impossible to shout recriminations at Freda. Andy searched the scorched grass for the missing joint. Suddenly inspired, he disappeared and quickly re-emerged from the kitchen with a bag of ice-cubes. On his knees again, he scrabbled and tossed his hands through the blood-splattered lawn.

"Got it!" he gasped.

"Gimme—quick!" said Madeline tremulously, closing the lumps of ice gently around the thumb.

"There now!" said Andy, satisfied. For a split second they were all quiet. Crickets croaked rhythmically in the long grasses beyond the garden wall. They watched as the white roof of an ambulance arched over the brow of the hill.

Ice was the one thing the thumb didn't need, the hospital doctor briskly snapped. Frostbite could make it virtually impossible to graft.

"We can try," he suggested in kinder tones.

"Oh Jesus," Andy bit his knuckles. "She'll have to learn to write with the left hand. Damn!"

He struck the wall of the casualty ward with the full force of his fist. Madeline was raging. She wanted to thump him herself. Another bloody cock-up, a potential mess resulting from good intentions.

He had found himself, he'd informed her only a few nights before, had finally discovered freedom. In Germany. Freedom. That's what he called it. After twelve years, just when she'd come to her own conclusions about marriage. Andy, Zoë and Madeline. A unit of three.

In the later seventies, when they used to discuss ideas, when they had friends who discussed ideas, they had voluntarily granted a mandate that would (in theory) permit each to breathe independently of the other. Childless for longer than intended, they'd led busy committed lives. Much of what they despised lay about them—the new bourgeoisie with its aggressively-styled dogmas which centred on progress, jobs for the boys (and girls, they had to remind themselves), the breeding of ill-controlled families, people who had gradually sold out, reformed university socialists now considering sending their sons to Clongowes.

They could live with that, they decided, without having to accept it. They had successfully by-passed a lot of disillusionment. Or so Madeline had thought, especially when they got Zoë. Zoë was the result of a working-holiday in Laos some five years previously, an adoption which had been costly as well as the best thing that had ever happened. Having joined the ranks of the Brat Brigade, both had inevitably developed some of the long-scorned traits of diehard parenthood. Andy, for one thing, belonged to the modern pram-pushing breed of men, something done matter-of-factly but with pride.

At the hospital she thought back to the journey. To reach the village they'd had to travel up the Mekong with the priest, a yellow-skinned Frenchman in long cotton pants and a short-sleeved shirt.

"C'est beaucoup plus loin?" Madeline had asked hesitantly, perspiring in the humidity.

"Bah non, pas trop," he replied, not looking at her directly.

"Comment la mère, est-elle morte?" Andy ventured, not wanting to appear too familiar with their taciturn companion.

"Je n'en sais rien," the priest had shrugged. "Je ne pose jamais des questions moi."

"Et le père?"

"Lui, il aurait pu être Français. Avec quelques-uns

d'entre eux, il est vachement difficile de savoir où ils se trouvent."

They asked little else, nervous of seeing this baby for the first time, a feeling sharpened by the sheer dimensions of the river, the strange, swollen brown-green pulsing stream which bore them onwards, the sense of darkness behind the simmering swamp-tangle on both banks. Madeline was bursting with anxiety, the recollection of a film called *The Killing Fields* flashing mentally in images of protruding bone, split skulls—bodies, floating on that waterway, the smell of war.

After such anticipation, meeting the child was a relief. It worked. Everything. They brought her back triumphantly, deliriously happy that they had taken the risk.

She had brought Zoë and the dog to the airport to greet him on his return from Germany. The first embrace was the best thing about the week that ensued. The dog pranced, Zoë pranced, Madeline waved frantically across the crowds until she caught his eye. He'd lost weight, and it suited him. He seemed relaxed, more handsome than ever. She realised, that in his absence, neither Zoë nor the dog, nor the visitations of various friends amounted to much. But she also realised that she was a wife with a capital *W* when the suspicions began. Every time he phoned he'd come from either a wine-tasting or a party. Another time he announced his plans for a cycling trip with somebody called Maria-Angela from Italy. With each letter and phone-call, her curiosity intensified. She knew the scene, had taken a couple of language courses over the years, well aware of the quenching surge of liberation which accompanied one's spouse-free movements after the first few days, when group dynamics and degrees of friendly contact with the other participants had been established. She knew all about the wine-tastings, the group activities, the cultural outings. Remembered the jostling Italian girls, always late for class, made up to the nines, the correct Americans, the French, slightly aloof. In Berlin she'd paired off with a young Yugoslav woman with a passion for *deutsche Literatur* and together they'd undertaken an enthusiastic foraging through every bookshop within a radius of five miles, had intense, indulgent discussions about Life and the Purpose of Existence. She knew what it was to be slightly drunk, to feel unfettered, released by the sheer mental space which a new environment and interested strangers created; she had met people who occasionally approached her as she sat on the street terrace of the Cafe Möhring, or wandered across Breitscheidplatz, bells from the Gedächtniskirche turning the air to something bordering on joy. It was good to have such time out from life, to absorb the world, the dossers and the doers, the sight of so much that was actual, yet slightly different.

So was she supposed to feel grateful that he told her whom he was with, without prompting, where he'd been and what he'd done? Was the succession of women's names, trotted off so casually, intended to appease her? One morning he phoned at seven-thirty, having forgotten to call the night before because Maria-Angela, a talented contralto obliged to learn German in order to sing Wagner on the international circuit, had given a recital at the institute, which was

179

followed by yet another party, at which more wine had been drunk. And all the phone-kiosks in Regensburg were occupied by Japanese tourists.

Since his return, the hunter restored, the word "freedom" had been bandied about accusingly and with uncomfortable frequency in various conversational combinations. Men wanted it every way, Madeline thought. Jam on their bread. It all came out while Zoë was in hospital, a gradual spilling and sorting out of conflicting emotions. The dismantling and rebuilding and further dismantling of private armouries as they fought and bickered, made love, fought and bickered in a private, cyclical war.

"For the first time in years," he told her firmly one morning at breakfast, "I've found my freedom. I've discovered that I'm confident, that people like me, that people are interested in what I do, what I say and I like it that way!" Madeline shifted, irritated by the litany. "I see. You've never experienced those things with me. I've never been interested in you. I don't enhance your confidence. I bring you down." Her temples throbbed with indignation.

"Some of the time you *do* bring me down," he replied, resisting her ironies. She slammed her cup onto its saucer. Another bargain-striking session, Andy's Home Truths. It would be a hot day. She was sick of the heat. While he was away, they had moved from bedroom to bedroom trying to find the coolest nocturnal nest, took imaginary journeys late at night down the Mekong, Zoë fingering the delta on the map, humming as she followed the river back to its source. The heat reminded her of Laos. Cicadas instead of crickets, gekos, bleached grass at the edge of the compound, the women who'd looked after Zoë watching them, watching her, carefully. For what? Signs of rejection, signs of racial superiority? The do-gooder, white cause-embracers come to remove a child from their culture, the place they knew? Her hands shook now as they'd shaken then. Perceived rejection, suspicion, distrust eroding her world.

"Wonderful stuff," she said cynically, running her thumb compulsively along the curve of the cup-handle, itching to fling the coffee at him.

"You walk in here after a month of the high life and lecture me on new-found freedom."

She said it resentfully, remembering his almost paternalistic control in earlier years, his unthinking assumption of responsibility for everything from driving to cooking. None of which, she now realised, he did particularly well.

"You make me sick," she said, hoping to provoke a response. His face was expressionless, almost quietly confident.

"You yammer about freedom as if you've been imprisoned."

He didn't react.

"It's as if you're blaming every disappointment on me," she said, more quietly. "That's what annoys me. The piety of it, the convenient hypocrisy. Oh yeah, that suits…" She paused automatically to refill their cups. "You really must have been the star attraction over there."

"It's one of the best things I've ever done."

"Well maybe you should've stayed there," she said sourly. "I wonder how long your precious freedom would last with whoever you were with."

That was it. She knew. Unspoken. There *had* been somebody. He had simply flowered in another direction. Anybody would in the circumstances.

"Jesus!" he roared, suddenly pacing up and down the floor, "I wish to God I was back in Germany, I wish I'd never come home, it's all spoiled!"

He thudded the kitchen door with his fist in the familiar gesture of frustration, and his mouth trembled. She ran to him then, and in a split second knew it was to thump him, not to comfort. "I've been here with Zoë for a month...working non-stop..." she gasped, struggling for breath, fists urging themselves to greater strength, "and you're whining about the wonderful time you had and how much you resent being back."

She drew back suddenly. She'd missed him terribly. But there hadn't been any lightning revelations in Dullsville. "There's no point expecting me to share the high because I can't and I feel nothing but... betrayal."

Andy arched an eyebrow. "That's a bit dramatic, isn't it?"

Just about everything which could conceivably go wrong, did go wrong. Murphy's Law. An electricity strike the week after he left, followed by a thunderstorm which knocked the phone out for two days and terrified Zoë, during which she missed a vital publishing commission. Then the job-hunting adolescent whom she'd paid to see to the lawn had insisted on mowing it on the wrong setting, sulkily, despite her entreaties. All followed by sleepless nights. Birds squawking and cackling at five in the morning, the sun slicing through the bedroom's white muslin curtains, bright as midday, the grain-drier on a neighbouring farm churning with a broken silencer from six o'clock. There had been a flat tyre on Chapelizod Bridge at rush hour, and as usual she couldn't unscrew the nuts herself. Sometimes, she thought privately, the best thing a woman could be was helpless. The easiest at any rate, the most hassle-free. Make no statements on freedom, not as a woman, proclaim ignorance of the workings of cars, lawn-mowers, electricity sockets and other people's minds.

She couldn't do that of course. She was too competent. She was also too impassioned with love for Andy, however jealously inadequate, however immature that love might be; the mere image of him enjoying the company of another woman in her absence driving her insane with a mixture of despair and arousal. It was hard. Difficult to possess someone through love without setting up borders and forbidden territories, without trying to own.

But he had betrayed something—their past and their ideals—not because of anything which might have happened in Germany but because he had clearly decided that she was now The Wife, a stiff-backed matriarch who granted favours and knew nothing about fun. He had forgotten what she believed, that she too could fight to preserve what was precious, in the depths of her being loathed the smugness of the middle-class east-coast Irish marriage. Rejected stripped pine and wicker baskets piled with fruit and vegetables significantly poised on stone-floored, recently installed, old-style modern kitchens, teak and mahogany cupboards, rococo tables shining and dead. As if there were no rain-forests, as if the entire planet didn't need to breathe collectively. She detested people who drove the length of the country in the search for the necessary alternative like an all-Irish non-denominational coeducational school, who piously unearthed trendy names for the newborn. The country was awash with Oisins, Fionns, Sinéads, Ciaras and a rising league of Beibhinns.

But Andy had mentally shelved her, had seemingly decided that her passions were too ideological, too social. Dull. As if dullness mattered in the face of what was urgent. If Zoë was to have a future.

They made love more than ever, every confrontation likely to be temporarily resolved by an attack on each other's bodies which was as heightened as it was surprising, laced with angry kisses, vigorous strokings and clingings, as if lives even beyond their own depended on such struggle, half in and out of clothes, curiously absorbed in another attempt at shaping.

Later that day they visited the hospital. The graft had taken. Zoë sat perched against a mound of pillows, her right forearm bandaged heavily, splinted, monstrous in proportion to her size. The sight of her brought them rushing to the bed, the morning scene forgotten.

"How is it darling?" Madeline asked, her eyes searching the child's face for signs of discomfort. Zoë smiled, revealing five-year old stubby teeth. Andy stroked her blue-black hair.

"She's more lovely than anything we could have produced ourselves," he murmured.

"Am I lovely Daddy?" Zoë asked carefully.

"Yes. Absolutely lovely."

She reached towards Madeline with her free hand, fiddled with the buttons on her shirt. "Abzooloot-lee...abzoolootlee love-lee..." she half-sang.

"She's still a bit doped," said Madeline.

"I'm not a dope!"

"Of course not darling. That's a different word. You're a clever, brave girl. That's what you are!" said Madeline approvingly.

"Here's a pressie," said Andy, taking a package from his pocket.

"Oh goody!" the child exclaimed. "You open it Mamma?" she asked Madeline. It was a small atlas.

He geared down at the Salmon Leap bridge. Looking down, the river reminded her again, algeous and low-flowing in the heat. The Mekong would be at its most swollen.

"We'll have to bring her back in a few years," she remarked.

"If she wants," said Andy frowning.

"She probably will want to. Out of curiosity if nothing else. The identity thing will have to be dealt with."

"You're right," he conceded.

It was what they accepted. That Zoë must see the other country. That she might return to her blood-culture within the next twenty years. For good. Zoë obsessed by her origins. It happened. With careful handling on their part, with honesty, it might never be an obsession. And all children, sooner or later, went away. An instinct came to bear, eventually. Spurn the parent, cut free, move out to the world, be absorbed. What counted was how that moving out evolved, that approach to the world. Madeline wondered if Zoë's would be desperate, fired by a negative image of herself in their sanitised Western culture. Or would it be the instinct of all children grown to adulthood, a natural searching for the future, for continuity? Yet there would be no future unless the past was acknowledged, roots touched, sifted through, unless blood-parents and grandparents could at least be imagined.

"She's happy, though," Madeline said, as they turned into the lane that led to their house. The old Fiat jolted along the potholes.

"Sometimes I think this is the end of the bloody earth," said Andy as he took the car along its pothole avoidance slalom-course. "We don't exist!" They waved at a neighbour, a new peace between them.

"Maybe we should move...emigrate," said Madeline.

"Maybe. D'you want to?" He glanced questioningly at her.

"It depends."

They pulled in as a tractor passed. To the left the huge grain fields shimmered pale brown. Threshing had begun further down towards the main road. The bales lay like giant coins, brilliantly tight and golden, the smell of barley and wheat enriching dusty air that wafted through the car windows. This was Ireland, part of it. The place they had chosen. It was Zoë's place too, Zoë, who spoke with an Irish accent and cursed in Hiberno-English, who knew lots of Irish words and a few German ones. Who did not, at this point, understand anything of Laos although she knew it concerned her. Who would probably never speak Lao.

The phone rang as they entered the hall. Madeline answered. A woman's voice (distinctly Italian) asked for Andy. She passed him the receiver, then belted upstairs, making as much noise as possible so that he'd know she wasn't listening. Him and his bloody space and freedom. Hadn't they gone to the ends of the earth for space and freedom. The only place they'd found it was in Zoë. She slammed the bathroom door and went to wash her teeth.

"That was Maria-Angela," he said some minutes later, following her upstairs.

"Oh. What'd she want?"

"She's moved. Just letting me have her new address—I've written it down." Of course, she thought. There would be a succession of letters for a while, the occasional phonecall.

"Good idea. Keep it with the others." She must try to be generous. To give him space. Whatever it was he felt he had missed that she hadn't. Andy and Zoë. They were all that mattered in a world of fractured ideals, of dreams too easily broken by tyrant principles. The result could be found in the rivers, where the corrupt remains of the dead were filtered, secreted in dark, tropical depths.

When the phone rang a second time, it was the hospital. Zoë could come home in two days time. The doctor apologised for having missed their visit.

"Will she be able to write?" Madeline asked.

"Sure thing. In any language." The young intern laughed.

They hugged each other with relief, still frayed by the memory of the child's pain and fear, her body taut with terror at the sight of her own blood that day. When they made love again, suddenly, Madeline knew that they were a family. Not the hated, dreaded kind, but a small tribe which was part of a bigger one, who would always fight for what must be protected. She knew other things too, that would have to be dealt with. Things that Andy would discover.

A Beast of a Man

T he usher had to ask him to leave. James looked around, startled, aware suddenly of pin-lit slopes of empty seats, crisp bags still crackling in the silence, the salty breath of popcorn hanging in the air.

"Sorry," he mumbled, gathering his raincoat and pad. The usher appraised the empty page, observed the mesh of doodles in one corner, stiffened instinctively. A bloody critic. Not that he cared much for cinema himself, but a job was a job, and he wanted to keep his. You never knew with intellectuals and newspaper people. You just never knew what went on.

James was slow to move. The usher stood there patiently, determined to see him out of the place.

"Some film," he remarked to the fellow, who flicked his torch on and off compulsively, even though the place was well-lit now in its desertion. The usher shrugged his shoulders, a half-respectful smile threatening to break on his tight-pressed lips. James could see that he wasn't going to commit himself to an opinion in the presence of a literary elder and better. Sod it, he thought. The old occupational hazard, the almost physical spasm which struck some people when it dawned on them that a critic had asked their opinion, the rigid unspoken hostility, the fear. He should be accustomed to it after fifteen years on the job. All the same, on days like this it still tried his patience, days when the need to engage somebody— anybody—in conversation about what he'd just witnessed was almost urgent.

Years of newsroom rationale, the transient atmospherics of which ensured that nothing, but nothing, was urgent outside the moment in print, in which word-value endured at the most for twenty-four hours before surrendering to immediate death, had curbed slightly that tendency to be swept along by the excitement of something, to permit the blooming of flagrant emotions. His reviews were by now notorious for their clipped precision, the absolute refusal to get embroiled in the hip literary vocabularies of his contemporaries. He was known as Carver, a remote reference to the great American short story writer of that name, but equally an innuendo concerning his capacity to hack something to pieces.

He stood up, loathe to leave the place until he had dragged some response from the usher. What he thought, mattered in some peculiar way. He was swamped with feeling, overpowered. Two hours of flooding, tumescent fascination. The book had been one thing, but the film was something quite different altogether, would bring the latent pederasts out in droves once the word got around, would disturb decent men and plant doubts in the minds of decent women. He had almost cried out as Humbert Humbert had manipulated his unknowing nymphet across his knee and into a position from which he could derive maximum sensation with the minimum of movement. As the girl's thinly clad posterior rolled back against Humbert Humbert's stomach, the camera cut to his face. It was all there, the furtive ecstasy, the spurting moment when he took her and she never even knew it.

Absinthe, Heloise, Angele, Cleo, Leonora, Lolita. And Brigid. Who were the people who wrote about such girls, who were they really? His body had frozen in the manner of most people in audiences faced with titillation, secretly awakening to fullest attention. Detachment was impossible. The air in the cinema flickered with colour, the spectra of shifting scenes, light, broken prismatically across the broad screen. Yet it was blue, the bluest, most beautiful light he had ever seen, his every muscle tensing, catching the density, the exquisite bloom of Humbert Humbert's desire, and then the attenuation, the gradual dissolution of the world he had dared enter.

"Have you actually watched it?" he addressed the usher in one final attempt at self-absolvement, by way of conveying the enormous impact which this film had made. It was an attempt to remove himself quietly, intellectually from some feared, inner monster. The usher regarded him with obvious distaste.

"Only bits."

"You should watch it all, it's worth it," James pressed, moving away from the man, down the red-carpeted steps toward the exit. The usher followed matter-of-factly, avoiding any point of debate or contact by deliberately casting his torchlight along the length of each row.

"Not my kind of thing that," he called pointedly.

"Not my kind of thing that," James mimicked him mentally, his head swaggering a little as he emerged from the central exit downstairs into the broad light of late July. Young people drifted in waves up and down O'Connell Street. It was ten o'clock, the last long rays of sunlight cutting softly down the length of the city centre, capping the sullen green head of the Anna Livia fountain. He pulled his raincoat on, though the night was warm, part of him wanting shelter, needing concealment, turning from any exposure, strangely vulnerable as he speeded on foot down to the office. Copy deadline eleven thirty. "Pervert. Bastard. Filthy, dirty, evil-minded, lascivious, inhuman wretch." That's what they'd call him, had he ever dared, were he to take the considerable risks of a man like Humbert Humbert. The nymphets were out in full force, twelve to fourteen-year olds whose parents either didn't care or about whose whereabouts they didn't know. Shameless little creatures, most of them, bobbing up and down the city streets, in and out of pubs and cinemas and burger-joints, their cigarettes lit, hair gelled or spiked, only their slender hips betraying their true age. Amoral, yet totally, totally, sweetly innocent. Somewhere in the centre of his being he cried out again. As he turned down the oil-slicked side street towards the back entrance of the newspaper, his heart split with recognition.

One of them—no more than thirteen—stared at him from the bus-stop opposite, aware of his penetrating, stricken glance. There was even a special telephone line for nymphets in distress, reports were filed on people like him, people who followed their inclinations. It was a criminal offence. He turned from her hostile little stare, her well-tutored young glance and burst through the fire-doors into the building.

Mentally, he listed the names, desperately, names that rolled effortlessly with his desire, reminding him. Absinthe, Heloise, Cleo, Leonora, Lolita. And Brigid. Lovely little Brigid. They would all grow up to be what society deemed "well-adjusted", normal, they would marry reasonable men, the majority of them, would know nothing, not ever, of the union of happy souls, would be sour before they were forty as their men betrayed them, or as they gradually betrayed themselves. The truth, he knew, was in the arms of girl-women. Unprintable. Taking the stairs in twos, his mind lingered on Brigid. He deliberated for a moment. The console awaited his trim thoughts. Carefully, dodging the minefields of words which waited to explode at the touch of a finger, he began to type the review.

⁂

No, no, we had a great time, honestly, really great. I mean we went all over the place, simply everywhere and it's not what you think at all. Uncle James is terrific fun, he bought me all kinds of things on the days we stopped off in places. Germany I liked best of all, driving on the right and all that, Uncle James knew everything about how to get around and speaks four languages fluently. He's a bit of a polylot really— polyglot I mean. Sorry.

No, it wasn't too bad. *That* end of things was easy not to think about too much. It didn't hurt at all, honestly, Uncle James was so kind and I did enjoy watching him sleep afterwards, though that didn't happen very often because I was so tired myself that I just passed out the moment he'd finished what he was at. Men are funny, aren't they? But the few times I watched I remember his beard, and how shiny and clean it was, and the way his funny thick eyebrows used to get a bit disorderly after we'd been in bed for a while. I have a lovely collection of foreign dolls now. He knew I liked those little ones with the bits of white lace and the lovely colours of their embroidered skirts and dresses and the—now what did he call them—*dirndls*—yes, that's what he called them. He even bought me a complete outfit for myself when we were in Bavaria, and the following day we went walking in the hills below the alps. It was a Sunday and some of the women we met were wearing theirs, so I felt just like a German woman. O how lovely, how fantastic it was! I felt like, I mean really *brill*, grown-up and free and able to do what I liked. That's one thing about him, whatever I wanted he let me have. Or do. I used to get a bit bored, just driving around so much, and anyway the holiday hadn't been my idea, it was his and after Dad died—well, everybody thought it might be a good idea, you know how grown-ups carry on and talk as if you weren't there and couldn't understand anything. "She's at a very impressionable age," Aunt Sarah—that's Uncle James's wife—said. That was a few months after the funeral. "It would do her good to see a bit of the world," someone else had advised Mum. "James is like a father to her, isn't he?" That's what Mum's brother Joe had said. What a laugh. Well yes and no.

In a way it's true.

I do love Uncle James, and it's just not fair what's happening to him. After all we didn't mean any harm and he was so nice to me always. I can't understand why he worried so much about things when we were away. Gosh. He nearly died when I told him the things I knew. He thought I'd done nothing, that I was a real greenhorn about you-know-what and that he'd have to show me everything. But he got a right land when he discovered that I knew what to do. I mean, they must have done what we did when they were at school too. I mean, Jane Delaney and me practised kissing and things in the classroom after school. Far better fun than homework I can tell you. Not that I felt anything much. I never have yet. But that doesn't matter. It's all fun anyway. Then Jane and me got Tommy Dalton to bend down so's we could photograph him. That was a laugh. I pretended to her that there was a film in the camera and she nearly died of fright for a week until I told her it was all a joke. Even funnier, Tommy won't come near either of us, because we never told him there wasn't a film in it, isn't that gas?" He goes absolutely *puce* any time he sees us, runs the other way. And his thingy was so teeny-weeny, really funny looking.

I don't think I've ever seen Uncle James turn puce, or get embarrassed about anything. Well, perhaps once. In that hotel in Belgium, a kind of motel in the Ardennes. We'd been making quite a racket, messing around beneath the quilt and all that. Uncle James had made a bit too much noise and I told him to put a cork in it and he put his hands over my mouth and nose, really fast like, I don't think he meant to smother me, but he nearly did and I kicked and thumped and finally managed to bite his fingers. He didn't say a word in reply when I cursed at him and told him to sod off somewhere else, that there was no need to kill me. That was the one time I saw him go a funny sort of pink, he closed his eyes for a moment I think, and then put his hands to his ears as if he didn't want to hear something. But there was nothing else apart from my voice. He pointed to the wall then, signalling. What he was really afraid of, was that there'd be somebody in the next room, and that people might find out. I still don't know what all the fuss is about. As I said, he bought me lots of things and gorgeous yummy dinners and taught me all about wines, well— a bit about wines—he was strict like that and wouldn't have me drunk or anything. But the dinners! And the desserts! He said he couldn't understand how I didn't turn into a little pig, that I really was a little pig, what with all I tucked away, so I ribbed him back and said that I was young and that's why I didn't turn into a pig. *Touché* he said. Now I know what that word means. I learnt so many new words from Uncle James. Unusual ones that mean ordinary things but sound so much nicer and interesting when you let your tongue fiddle over them. *Vulnerable, potent, nubile, extraordinary* (he'd break it into two parts, not like people here who use it like one word and leave out the "a" of "extra"), *infinite, cosmic, cinematic, treatment, urbane, profane, hedonistic, heterosexual, chastity, innocence, experience, intention.*

Having the right experience was everything, Uncle James said. And the word intention did not mean the same thing as "intend" or "what-was-your-intention-when-you-took-that-young-girl-off-on-holiday?" It meant all the layers of meaning in any feeling, word or deed, and he made me learn that and remember it, because he said I'd need it, that the time would come when understanding what he called the *intentionality* of experience would stand to me. Talking about that sorta stuff, did anybody ever teach *you* about intentionality?

I became a woman when I was with him, except that I forgot all about periods and things and for a while thought he'd done me an injury and nearly died of fright. But he sorted me out and told me not to worry, that it was a great occasion and something to be very proud of. So off we went out to dinner in this special place that evening, outside Rothenburg, I wore my new *dirndl*, and I had really juicy turkey and lots of pickles, and masses of asparagus and teensy-weensy little new potatoes with lovely sweet bits of pink cabbage trailing through them. After, I had a mountain of ice-creams, pink, yellow and dark chocolate with hot chocolate sauce running all hot and sticky down the sides. And he let me taste my first glass of wine as a special treat. Just a little, he said in his daddy-ish way. But the wine wasn't all it's cracked up to be, a bit sour if you ask me. He said not to say that or the restaurant owner would be sour. Tart was the word, or very dry, or acidic, but never, ever, sour. Then he sort of chuckled to himself.

A week later he took me on a giant wheel. That was in Vienna. In *Wien* as the Austrians call it. That's pronounced "veen," by the way. Anyway that was an absolutely brilliant experience, chock-full of intentionality too. We hopped in, just the two of us, it was a wettish Monday and all the school-kids were in school and all the oldsters at work or something, so we had the whole basket to ourselves though there were some touristy types above and below us. Anyway it took off and wow-ee was that something else. It rose up quickly over the city and I've never seen anything so beautiful in all my life, because even though it was wet, the sun was shining behind us and broke through the sheets of rain and everything, everything was sopping wet and kind of golden in that light, all the red roofs and churches and lonely spires and the little ones like onions or bulbs. "O Uncle James I love you!" I shouted when we stopped at the top, at the very tip-top of the wheel and of the world, and I could tell by his face that he was madly happy, him and his funny old ways, because his eyes became all soft and glistening. To tell you the truth I thought he was going to cry and I don't know what the hell I'd have done because I mean the idea of men crying—that's kind of *outré*, isn't it—ha! Another word he taught me!

I saw absolutely loads and loads of films with Uncle James too, because he said he had to do a little work while on holiday, but most of them were pretty boring stuff, and some of them were just weird, not what you'd see here, but all the same he was very particular about what I saw, nothing that would, as he put it, corrupt my mind.

It's really funny being back here, what with all the fuss and so on, because Uncle James is one of the nicest people you could meet and we just like one another so much, we get on like real mates. He says that I should never let anything or anyone spoil my vision of life (whatever that means). Well, I think I know what he means. And he says there's an awful lot of mullarkey going on about how people should behave and what's moral and proper and normal but all the time men and women are killing one another with disappointment and hate, and forget how to love one another honestly. No, I've nothing else to say, and you can put those stupid dolls back in the cupboard because they're ridiculous and I'd rather tell you in words than by sticking that stupid-looking long thing into the girl-doll. Because that had very little to do with it, even though things did happen. There was much more to it. Honestly.

&

Arra, God help the little girleen, shure isn't it a pity of her, getting mixed up with a fella like that, oh a cute bucko if ever there was one, thon buck comes from a good family but you'd wonder what happened to himself at all at all. Highly respected he was too, held down a fine job with that paper for years. How could he do such a thing, I ask you darling, here have some more coffee, what a beast of a man, oh of course some of these young gels ask for it, out strutting and performing from the age of ten and they know what they're doing, it's in the blood m'dear, in the blood. Women. Daughters of Eve the lot of them, should be forcibly exorcised every year from the age of ten. It's the bleeding does it, makes them hot. That brat must have led him astray somehow, it's at home doing her homework she should have been, or tucked up in her bed, or helping her Mammy with the dishes like any normal daughter would. Oh Mother of God and the Eternal Saints and Blessed Saint Jude of the Banana

Republic, and St Jerome of the Mountain and Maria Goretti, where are ye now when yere blighted children need ye, what's the world coming to at all at all, that poor little child, that poor, poor, lost, lonely, helpless little waif, with no Daddy, shure these things happen at the best of times and there's not a thing to be done about them, all we can do is hope and pray. The Lord knows she needs all the prayers she can get, as does your man, shure God help him there's probably some little want there, and you know what men are like. Filthy, dirty animals, the lot of them, they'd get up on a gust of wind if they could, filthy, perverted, creatures by nature, I read once about this Italian woman doctor who was raped and taken advantage of by a young fellow and didn't she manage to slip him something after the event, in a drink like, and while your man was out for the count didn't she heave-ho the trousers offa him, give him the aul' snip-snip like, and Bob's your uncle that's the last time he'll attempt anythin' like that. That's what them boys needs, a bit of the rough stuff, but of course the women are as bad, whores, fat cunts the lot of them, out for what they can get, out to bleed a normal man dry, out to trap the best normal men into impossible situations, but arra, God help the little girleen, shure isn't it a pity of her, how will she ever lead a normal life now, getting mixed up with a fella like that? Oh a cute bucko if ever there was one...Oh a cute bucko if ever there was one...Oh a cute bucko if ever there was one...

Minerva's Apprentice

Being locked up with all those other females had something to do with it. You knew that and so did Marika. Only three months beforehand you would have given an arm and a leg to be flown to Los Angeles to meet your favourite Monkee, Davy Jones. Los Angeles. Place of angels and palm-trees. Where girls your own age wore mini-skirts up to their backsides and high suede boots in spite of the heat. Where he lived and sang. Only three months beforehand, before you went to boarding-school you would dawdle outside the house in the evenings and gaze west at runnels of pink cloud, just when the first bats began to wheel about, when everything of promise was just over the hills and westwards across the sea.

Things changed after meeting Marika. Within a month you had started to pal around together because you both read the relevant pages of *The Group* by Mary McCarthy, within two you had both admitted that Sister Brigitta was certainly a different class of a nun, and by November there was no doubt but that it was love. Nor was this something to worry about. Marika, who was precocious and brilliant and had read about that kind of thing, assured you that it happened to girls of a certain age. None of which prevented her own absorption, or deflected her in the slightest from the love object who taught you both English. Nuns still held a bit of mystery in late 1967, hadn't quite thrown their veils and habits to the luscious winds that blew in the wake of Vatican II, despite the call for ecumenism, the songs of love and freedom, despite the Beatles discovery of the Maharishi and the mystic East.

She was unlike any Brigid-type you'd ever known before. Sure, you'd heard about Saint Brigid, who vied in your mind for popularity of place with Saint Patrick. With his driving out the serpents and her founding a great monastery in County Kildare, his shenanigans with the shamrock and her cross-weaving, the cause of Christianity had been furthered in the country. Such were the mites which nestled in glorious forms of misrepresentation in your brain. Other Brigid-types you'd met previously were not much to write home about. There was Sister Brideóg, who'd taught you in primary school and caned half the class for not being able to recite "Sráideanna Baile Átha Cliath" by heart. There was also a Sister Brídín, little Bridget, a coy version of the great name, who ruled benignly and trustingly in History class, unaware that serious day-dreaming could be got on with as she rambled and ranted *as Gaeilge* about the glories of the past. Then there was your grandmother Bridget, the most interesting of the lot, who kept every issue of *Ireland's Own* for you long after you'd lost interest in Kitty the Hare, and ate an egg a day straight from the shell. You too were Bridget but hadn't a clue where you came from or where you were headed, preoccupied with blushing and hauling your changing body into some sort of order each day.

Mostly the Brigid-types were plain as porridge. But this Brigitta was absolutely ravishing, an almost Scandinavian Kriemhild for whom any knight would be only too glad to unearth hidden treasure and golden torques. You being a sucker for looks and mystery, deprived of information on Davy Jones the Monkee, could not help respond. Marika would link your arm as the two of you strolled around the convent park which followed the outline of the crannóg lake nearby. In the new year, when the Donegal and Cork girls were killing themselves whacking a camogie ball, getting broken noses, glasses, teeth in the process, or when the Dublin lot were doggedly playing tennis in spite of the wind and the damp, the pair of you circled the park in the hopes of catching a glimpse of her, greeting nuns who passed you by, knowing they disapproved of the lack of healthy participation. You talked and talked. "Brigitta. Brigitta. Brigitta. Legs and a figure," Marika would hiss excitedly. "Oh God she's beautiful!" would come your rejoinder. And Marika, who considered herself fat and dumpy, a sack of potatoes, but who was no better or worse than anybody else who stuffed eight Kimberley biscuits into their mouths, or dug into slabs of fruit-cake and peanut-butter at elevenses, would rave on and on about Sister Brigitta's perfection, her high cheekbones, her high breasts, till by the time the tea bell sounded out across the lake and parkland, you were both in a state of distraction.

You began to compete for her praise. One afternoon

when the class results for the week were read out, you came top of the list for the third week in a row, with Marika a close second. Afterwards, she put her head between her hands in a gesture of despair and sobbed as if her heart had broken.

"For heaven's sake you'll make it up next week!" you said unsympathetically.

"That's not the point!" she snapped, blowing her nose before laying her head in her arms again. She didn't care who saw, and soon half the class had rallied around, offering comfort, so that you began to feel like a criminal.

What Marika said mattered. Her praise was important, her condemnation cut deeply. She was like Sister Brigitta herself. Her sphere of influence was greater than she realised. You remembered too well the day the Irish teacher had played back some recordings he'd made of your voices reading poetry. As your droning monotone murdered "Cúl an Tí" Marika laughed outright and set the whole class into paroxysms. You wanted to die. Hot-cheeked and smarting, you temporarily hated her.

But now you felt victorious. You knew how you had worked while Marika played court jester, imitating teachers and classmates with equal abandon, proclaiming contempt for the drones who did their homework. And still she managed to draw sympathy. You realised for the first time how gullible people are, how easily they respond to the obvious, what unjust judgements they make and how jealous they can be. That evening as you streamed down the glass arcade which separated the old part of the school from the new, into the study hall, you knew more certainly than ever that what Shakespeare and all the lads wrote was the most important thing in life, but that people were too lazy to think about it. An old nun called Sister Benedict was tending the geraniums which grew practically all year round in the arcade's glasshouse climate. The sun made the place warm and dusty, alive with the prickling odour of the plants. In an instant—whether it was because of the geraniums, or the deceptive yellow light that drifted warmly through the glass, or because you simply felt alive—you knew how you would spend your life.

That night, just as you'd settled into the routine of torchlight reading, there was a tug at the curtain which closed your alcove off from the dormitory corridor.

"Pssst!"

"What?" you asked archly, feeling independent, still slightly angry about Marika's blatant performance that afternoon.

"Can I come in?" she whispered urgently.

As usual you succumbed, too fond of her to refuse anything for long.

"Can I get in?" she added, whipping back the bedclothes before you had time to consider, then sliding between the sheets. Her feet were cold. Evidently there was something on her mind. You sensed a "Brigitta" heart-to-heart conversation in the offing.

"What're you at?" she demanded, reaching to see what you were reading.

"Leave it," you commanded, surprising yourself. Anything else but not that. There could be no intrusion on Hopkins's "Spring". To your quiet satisfaction she acceded, babbling about Sister Brigitta and wasn't it *awful* the way she had to peer through everybody's hair on Saturday nights to check for nits? Wasn't it bloody *awful*? You agreed but you loved it. The nun's hands were fine and pale and she had often admired your own hair which was thick, long and curling. You could have sat there for all eternity if anybody was fiddling with your hair, never mind the nun. You both giggled as you thought of the terrible tasks the novices had to undertake. One of them had been assigned to First Year fingernails, an inspection which took place every Monday morning before you left the dormitory. Then you lay on your backs, staring at the ceiling, and told a few jokes to pass the time.

"What's black and white and goes round and round?"

"I dunno," Marika replied sleepily.

"A nun falling down the stairs."

"Heard it before," she muttered, suddenly springing to life with one of her own.

"What's red and green and goes round and round?"

"Tell me."

"A frog in a liquidiser."

You both started to shake with laughter, holding the pillow to your mouths in an attempt to stifle it.

"Can I stay?" Marika asked in mock humility, knowing the ice was broken, wheedling her way into your favour again.

"Yes," you replied gruffly. You turned from her and you both lay back to back, snug as two animals in hibernation.

It was all around the school the next day. Uainín

O'Neill, a potential prefect if ever there was one, wore a pained expression and ignored you. Lying— "lurking" as Marika put it—in the alcove beside yours, she'd overheard the sniggering and snorting. Your own classmates were shocked. The second years passed remarks and made clicking noises whenever you or Marika passed, while the older girls had superior smirks. You made no explanations. Instead you laughed, brimming with the knowledge that already their minds were rapidly solidifying with fear and ignorance.

In early February the convent grounds seemed removed from the tawdriness of the world. Everything was white, misted, the lake-edge frozen, clumps of snowdrops like innocence snagged in hoops of pale sunlight. Mornings were freezing cold, there was Mass, followed by a breakfast of one sausage and as much bread as you could fit in your stomachs, the gabble of the Donegal Gaeltacht girls good-humoured and compliant even at that time of day. On Saturdays you sang in the choir, exalted in the high notes of "An Fuiseoigín San Spéir" or the "Jubilate Deo". Time was hurtling, like a wheel controlled by some only remotely-interested force. There was French and German with the teacher who had talked his way into the job by virtue of his loquaciousness and fluency in both languages but who had no qualifications. That was followed by Latin, a severe test of the nerves as Sister Valarian put you through your paces. After that Sister Conception explained the mysteries of the parabolic curve. And after that—English—truth in the day, blood in your body, radiance in the heart! Marika and you had made up completely since the night she slept with you, sat eager-beavered and in thrall as Sister Brigitta diverged from her usual fierce routine, strangely relaxed. The angers which streamed from her mouth at times were completely absent and there was no trace of the frustrated young witch who had occasionally referred to you collectively as a group of empty-minded vegetables. She regarded you as slightly unsavoury invaders into the sphere of some private contemplation. Nobody could say she had favourites. As a result, her anger was almost preferable to Sister Valarian's Latinate praises which usually centred on Marika, setting her apart from the great unwashed who couldn't identify a second declension noun in a month of Sundays.

"Today is what day, girls?" she greeted, her habit making a rip-rushing sound as she strode into the classroom with such energy that her rosary beads bounced.

"Come on—quickly!" she snapped.

"Saint Brigid's Day, Sister." somebody obliged.

"And what do we know about Saint Brigid?" she asked, sitting down for a change, laying her books neatly on the lectern desk.

"She was a saint," someone else muttered. The group tittered.

"That's en-ough girls..." she rapped the table warningly. Your eyes lingered on the length of her fingers, the delicate curve of the finger-tips, the white crescents at the base of her nails. You had never seen such lovely hands before. Then someone else said that her father had been a wealthy man, that Brigid had given his money to the poor and eventually became a nun whom everybody respected.

"Ah yes," Sister Brigitta mused thoughtfully, nodding her head as if that was what she'd expected to hear. For a moment her eyes grew distant, lost the slightly chill reserve with which you were so familiar. She told you about the real Brigid, a pagan goddess who lived centuries before the Christian woman, who was the equivalent of the Gaulish Minerva and whose pagan festivities on the first day of spring had been replaced by the Christian feast of St Brigid. The real Brigid was exceptional in every way, she said, looked after writers and artists throughout Europe and had been known to heal people who prayed to her.

"...and she was born at sunrise not inside a house and not outside it either—and she was fed from the milk of a red-eared cow..." she said, hypnotising you with the poetry of it. A shudder of disgust ran through the class.

"...and she used to hang her wet red cloak on the rays of the sun, and the house she lived in gave off a blazing light when seen from a distance..."

You suddenly remembered what your grand-mother had once said, and cut in quickly.

"And she spent her life guarding a sacred fire and there were no men allowed near it..." you added triumphantly.

For the first time she responded. It was as if your interjection had pulled her back from the tantalising frontier of some reverie you could only imagine.

"Excellent!" she said briskly in her usual tone of voice, although her expression betrayed mild surprise.

"Tell me about the fire," she instructed.

"What do you mean Sister?" you asked, your heart thudding in panic.

213

"The fire—what kind of fire are we talking about here?"

"I don't know."

"Guess child! What happened Fionn when he burnt his finger and tasted the salmon?"

"He became wise."

Incredibly, you were locked in discussion with Sister Brigitta, who had forgotten that English essays awaited comment, that there was a great deal of untidiness awaiting condemnation, and that, as usual, people would have forgotten to use paragraphs in order to indicate the development of ideas.

"So where does that leave you?" she asked, ignoring the rest of the class, hand tucked beneath her chin as she regarded you.

"The fire..." you began, "...the fire was the fire of knowledge and the reason men couldn't go near it..."

Again, you stabbed wildly for an answer, unwilling to make an eejit of yourself.

"...was because certain knowledge is for women only, maybe..."

You thought of your brother Manus, rampaging and pimply, like Plug in the *Beano*, and of the school chaplain, who was soft and unworldly and smelt of bacon and sausages.

"...and maybe the men mightn't understand it...and...and...things have to be looked after."

"What the fuck is she talking about? She's off her head! Come down to earth!" You could hear low whispers of ridicule simmering in the air. Even Marika was gaping.

"But sister what has that got to do with real life?" she demanded indignantly. Your face was hot, and your legs trembled as you stood there. You waited for Sister Brigitta to run your theories to ground.

"Where did you learn that?" she asked, smiling broadly.

"My grandmother was called Brigid and she told me things," you replied meekly.

"Aren't you the lucky girl to have a grandmother like that!" she exclaimed.

Marika's jaw dropped in mock disbelief. Reading, and the knowledge of myths and legends were all very well so long as they earned good marks in exams. She planned to become a famous doctor some day and took your idea of becoming a poet lightly.

"Who ever heard of a woman poet!" she'd once said scornfully, laughing at the idea of anyone scribbling verses in the dead of night, starving to death in a Parisian garret.

The hards got to work after class. "Don't forget your cloak! Or matches for the fire!"

"Well, well, well," Marika said teasingly, "there's at least one poem in this."

"Go to hell!" you grumbled, sick of the running commentary which was part of life in a boarding-school, the conformity which kept everybody in a state of permanent self-criticism. You knew that even that place, with its occult dawns and sunsets, the frozen stillness of the lake, the mysteries of bullrush and curlew, its mystical daily imagery, would be shed at least in part as time passed. The month of February was supposed to be a time for beginnings, for freshness. You felt it in your bones. By now you also realised that life without your champion, she who understood things so well, was unthinkable, the distinct possibility rearing its head that after she took her vows later in the year she would be transferred. What she understood about living you could only grope towards. You would brace yourself for the loss, would offer prayers and supplications to saints you didn't believe in, just in case anything could be done to avert disaster. Marika would join you in the church before Benediction, clasping her hands, gazing heavenwards with a devotion that would do credit to Jennifer Jones in *The Song of Bernadette*, the most recent film you'd seen in the school recreation hall.

By May you were close to dementia. News was out that Sister Brigitta was going to America to work with the hippies in San Francisco.

"Sure she knew next to nothing about hippies until we explained what they were to her!" said Marika haughtily, masking her disappointment.

It was difficult to imagine Sister Brigitta out there among the Flower People, but on the other hand you reasoned that it would be good for her to see the world and do her living somewhere more promising. Then someone else said that she was being sent on the African missions to teach in some Nigerian school. You didn't approve of the idea at all whilst admitting that she'd undoubtedly look fantastic in a white habit and would definitely win the hearts of all and sundry. Her arrival in such a place would be greeted by hundreds of singing black people who'd raise their hands in jubilation as she approached their village on a river-boat. But you opted for San Francisco, preferring the somewhat chancy notion of Sister Brigitta opening a hostel for lost hippies and gentle vagrants near Chinatown. In years to come you would follow her and become her helper.

The night before the novices took their final vows Marika couldn't sleep with worry. You suggested a trip to the trunkroom on the other side of the school, where the cases and assorted luggage of four hundred girls and fifty nuns were stored. You didn't wait until midnight for fear of falling asleep in advance, but hovered in the toilets which provided a good view of the nuns' nocturnal undressing activities, until no lights remained on, before slipping down the curving brown staircase, clutching at each other's dressing-gowns in nervousness. Crossing the arcade, the chill air caught your bare ankles, and the smell of polish mingled with that of geraniums.

You took a short-cut through a dormitory. None of the sleeping bodies stirred. Finally, beneath the eaves, high up on the third floor, was a linoleumed stairway which led to the attic. Torch in hand Marika eased her way through the narrow door, and you followed. The day had been reasonably warm, and the room smelt dry and musty. There was a sense of permanent stillness, the heavy tang of old leather, of things undisturbed by everyday matters. You rooted around quietly, checking the name-tag on each case and trunk, not knowing what to expect. Then you found it. Her name in religious life and her other name, her real name. And her address. She was from a seaside town further south, a small fishing village you'd once visited on a day-trip. Her real name didn't interest you, seemed less authentic than the one with which you were both familiar. Brigitta. Marika eased the trunk open. You noticed that her hands were trembling as you held the torch, but perhaps your hand was trembling. It was empty, except for a couple of sea-shells in one corner.

"Damn. Nothing," said Marika in disappointment. You stopped her from slamming the lid shut.

"There's these." You gestured at the shells.

"What use are they?" she almost wailed.

"What did you expect—letters?" you asked laconically, opening the trunk fully again. Marika stood like a tragic figure, aware that all was lost, that Sister Brigitta was leaving and that her trunk would soon be gone too. You deftly gathered the shells and counted them. Six in all.

"Three each," you told her. "Which do you want?"

She examined them slowly, as if choosing were vital. There were two scallops, three cockles and one conch. It was more simple than you'd anticipated. A scallop each, a cockle each, and you agreed to toss a coin for the conch the following morning. It didn't seem like theft. After all, she was leaving and it was only right that you should both have a keepsake, something to remember her by.

Naturally you were seen on your return journey to the dormitory. An insomniac nun was on the prowl, paused for a moment before an uncurtained window and spotted two figures creeping along the arcade at midnight. There was an enormous fuss the next day. Words like "deceitful," "untrustworthy" and "immature" were used with alacrity. Marika was labelled the ringleader because she was more vocal, you were castigated by your music-teacher for being "a sneaky little girl". But they didn't find the shells, and at least if Brigitta had noticed their absence when packing her trunk to leave, she hadn't told. They were very probably not supposed to have been there in the first place.

Finally, it was the beginning of June and the end of term. Paris was seething with angry students and people were talking about flying to the moon in the near future. The name Cohn-Bendit was on girls' lips, and Scott Mackenzie's song about San Francisco was still popular. The whole place fizzed with excitement at the prospect of the long holidays. Marika and you watched and sniffled as a tall figure with a black veil got into a car and was driven away, never to return. It was a golden evening, the horse-chestnut was all blossom and poise as you craned out over a window-ledge and followed the car down the curve of the avenue. Marika threw a tantrum later and was forbidden to watch *Top Of The Pops* in the final week of term. She didn't care. She was too distraught. That night you scrawled the first few lines of a poem, your hand hot and sweaty and nail-bitten, wanting to hang your wet cloak—if you had one—on the sun's rays, to keep the fire burning brilliant, knowing an arsenal of words could change much that was painful.

Strong Pagans

The church was in the old graveyard outside the town. It rested in a hollow, close to our family plot and also to the ornate obelisk on which multitudes of angels trumpeted over the Capriano plot. Tender tributes to the dead were inscribed beneath sepia-tinted photographs of fish- chip- and ice-cream-selling family members who had passed on to the great reward. Nearby was a life-sized statue of Christ the King, seated on a throne. We loved to sit on his knee and swing from his stiff neck, imagining beneficence.

"What reward?" Beth whined insistently.

"Oh—" I bluffed, "our reward in heaven; there'll be lots of goodies, stuff like that—"

"What goodies?" Anton asked, challenging me.

"Well—lots of whatever you want—and you won't have to look at people you hate," I explained.

"Does that mean Mrs Blundel won't be there?" said Beth. Mrs Blundel was our music teacher, a woman of venomous loquaciousness, who nicknamed every eleven-year-old in her care. Anton was called Specky Foureyes, Beth became Ducky Darling, Anna Capriano was known as Signorina Chips, while I struggled with Buckteeth.

"It's possible she might be," I surmised soberly.

"But we'd all feel different, so it wouldn't matter," said Anton.

"Perhaps." Beth was not consoled.

≈

We broke into the church one day close to Hallowe'en. The afternoon was warm enough to resuscitate any remaining flies, so that the first thing I remember after smashing the stained glass with a stone is the intense buzz of newly-awakened insect life from within.

"Come on!" I whispered to Anton and Beth, who hung back cautiously, Beth's expression shifting between horror and curiosity. Hanging on to the single bar which curved in front of the window, I reached down to pull her up.

"Push her Anton!" I hissed impatiently. She started moaning about the state of her shoes and that we'd all be killed when we got home but we ignored her, pulling and shoving to hoist her up.

"Now you," I commanded Anton, who sprang with greater agility than either of us and almost toppled us from the high sill. He banged at the glass panes with his elbow, the old lead lattice-work giving way easily. We were through.

We gaped for some moments, silenced by the atrocity we had committed as much as by the antique beauty of the empty church. Below us was the altar, deep and wide, mahogany topped with marble which was very white and only slightly veined. The pews had been removed a century ago, when a new cathedral was built to employ the famine-stricken and also when the need to flaunt a turreted, spired neo-gothic fortress on the highest point above the town seemed most urgent. There, too, it could serve the dual purpose of almost touching heaven and annoying Protestants. What remained here was a simple cream-walled rectangular space, at the back of which was a deep marble font, surrounded by small statues of the apostles and thronging angels. Above them, suspended by a fine chain, was the Holy Ghost in all his finery, golden rays sprouting from the dove form and directed at the font over which babies heads used to be doused with water.

Anton was the first to spring down to the altar.

"Crikey," he said, dropping nimbly to the floor. Beth and I followed but remained on the altar.

"What if we're caught?" she asked, before leaping to the floor.

"Don't be silly; we won't be," I replied, annoyed at any censure. Why did people always have to spoil anything interesting, I wondered. Why did they worry so much about doing the right thing, about being good?

"Nothing's going to happen," Anton calmed her from the floor of the church, his voice echoing around the arched wooden ceiling. Then he drew a tin whistle from underneath his jumper and tested it by hooting once or twice. The sound was thrilling. Beth and I begged him to play. He raised the instrument to his mouth and began to make sounds. It was nothing recognisable. I knew he was just messing, that this was nothing learnt at Mrs Blundel's musicianship hour, but it had rhythm and it gathered momentum, and his body swayed in harmony. It was then I began to love Anton, feelings of extreme fondness and affection flooding through me, because I recognised that our blood was the same, our inclinations rooted in something similar. I didn't fall in love with him for another fifteen years, by which stage I had stopped loving him. It took a long time for the two loves to flow as a single current, for us to discover who we are today.

I danced on the altar, my arms stretched high, fingers curved, limbs raised, back arched to the sound that flew to the full height of the roof. Beth looked on and smiled, regarding us as if from a distance— at least that's how I remember the moment when I sensed her incomprehension if not her disapproval of our antics. Turning and circling, I caught sight of the fresco depicting the ascent into heaven. It showed Christ in his purple robes. They flowed and shimmered around his feet so that I wondered how they stayed on. Cherubs and minute angels spun around him as if they too were dancing to Anton's music, happy and delirious with unnamed joy. The Holy Ghost hovered above his head in the way he always seemed to hang around people's heads, and high above was Michael the Archangel, brandishing a sword, his brow furrowed as he glared fiercely at a group of cowering pagans on the far side of the image, his hand pointing heavenwards. I began to grow dizzy, but Anton continued to play after I had collapsed flat out on the altar, my eyes drifting slowly over the ceiling. Only then did I notice the matted cobwebs, and also, more worrying, bats.

Just then, someone banged abruptly at the door. The fluted curve of the handle began to rattle.

"Who's in there?" a serious voice demanded

indignantly. We stared at one another. Beth's face was white.

"It's all right, don't cry," I said, pinching her arm slightly. She ignored me.

"Us," she replied.

"Who's us?" the voice demanded again. This time she remained silent because Anton held his hand tightly across her mouth while I grabbed her legs. She flailed at us angrily with both arms while we struggled to keep her quiet. Anton's eyes pleaded with me to do something. I shook my head vigorously, indicating silence. We remained like that for half an hour, by which time the voice, which I had recognised as belonging to my pious Uncle Bart, had taken itself elsewhere. By then the bats were flitting rapidly above us, Beth was sniffling and we knew it was time to leave. We shinned up to the high window again, pulling and shoving at Beth to lift her clear of the altar. It has always seemed to me that Beth was deliberately helpless then and still is, and that her reward has been a relaxed, orderly life.

Needless to say we were caught and punished. Uncle Bart, who frequently took a detour through the old graveyard after his evening prayers in the cathedral, had recognised Beth's voice, assumed that her brother and I were also present and reported accordingly to our parents. Anton and Beth are my third cousins, our parents were on reasonably friendly terms, and the four of them awaited us at my house when we breezed in casually as if nothing had happened. Beth got off the lightest, considered to be innocent and led astray by two extremely bold older children, Anton was whacked around the legs by his father, and I was thoroughly shaken and shouted at, my parents useless as ever when it came to doing anything firm or disciplinary. They went through the motions of being very cross just to show Beth and Anton's parents that they were not softies, and knew their duty. I have never been convinced that they did know their duty but I always loved them because they were so ineffective, because they spoiled me and because to my mind I was spoiled usefully in terms of my future.

Anton and I left school the same year and headed into different careers, if you could call mine a career. I spent one year in Trinity, failed everything but met people whom I considered to be interesting and worthwhile company, and I also joined the drama society. I was a regular in the various pubs up and down Nassau Street and Lincoln Place and got to know Anna Capriano, whose family still lived in our town and had sent her at great expense to do a course in dress design. Through her I got in touch with Anton again, because they were going out together and seemed to have a rather sullen, quaint relationship in which Anton conformed to the Italian mode of courtship. Most of the girls I knew were either passionately in love, trying to be passionately in love, or in the middle of a fraught break-up, with one of the poets who lectured us, flattered us and told us we had enormous potential, but then dropped us as soon as we began to believe it.

By then, I was not really interested either in Anna or in her oppressive family; my sights were fixed more firmly on Anton and I was fascinated by the apparent order and discipline of his academic life as an economics student. I'd imagined him doing something else, like music, arts or oriental studies, but never economics. He took a huge and unwarranted interest in Anna's work, something which charmed me and fitted my perception of him as a fluid, artistic, sensuous animal. He had grown handsome, slimly-built but firm, his hair was brown and wavy, the structure of his face and jaw Grecian in proportion. He was very much my aesthetic ideal. What of it if he had chosen economics, I would think, watching him help Anna select samples of material from the little pattern-books she kept in her bag, observing him finger the satins and velvets, and brush the soft wools with his fingers.

Beth remained at home to work in the local branch of an insurance office. She had never shown any inclination to move away and got married to a production assistant at the creamery some time after I failed the September repeats. They built a pleasant, airy house outside the town, and within two years her first child was born. Now she has five and her husband heads the production team and travels abroad to stroll around dairies and inspect yoghurt-making machines in Denmark, Germany and the Netherlands. They are a happy couple. He likes to assume control and treats her as if she was his daughter, but Beth has always liked being looked after, so she's lucky to have found someone who likes to do it. We meet at Christmas in one of the local hotels, when practically three generations of people who either left the town for Dublin or emigrated, return and attempt, over a drink, to re-establish points of contact. Those hours are full of "Do you remember?" and "Will you ever forget the time when...?", so it's natural that we almost always recall the day we broke into the church and danced on the altar. Of course, as Beth remembers it, she danced on the altar too; but that is not the case, she merely looked on. Even more surprising, she seems completely to have forgotten how Anton gripped and almost smothered her with his hands while I held her legs—perhaps that's as well.

"We had great fun then," she mused last Christmas, swirling her Dubonnet thoughtfully.

"Mmm," I replied vaguely, reluctant to remember.

"You were always imagining things," she said then, looking at me. I refrained from referring to her failure to imagine anything and forced myself to smile agreeably.

"Anton was as bad," I said, nudging him. She didn't like that. Even though we're married, she regards me even today as a a bad influence, someone who may have led him astray at a critical point in his development. Our failure to divide and multiply as she has done seems to reinforce her doubts. You only have to observe her with her own children to know that boys will be boys and will wear the trousers, while girls will sew, knit, cook and breed.

"He was impressionable," she replied, as if Anton's fall from grace must be explained. I held my silence, wishing he would speak for himself. Unexpectedly, he did.

"No, just a bit different," he said.

"You were impressionable," Beth insisted, her eyes darkening unexpectedly.

"I found what I was looking for, all the same," he

said. I glowed, linked my arm companionably through his, despite some discomfort at witnessing the mild frisson of disagreement between them.

"He found me!" I almost crowed at her, but she looked through me as if she hadn't heard.

That's the way our relationship has always been. It must be asserted, affirmed and reaffirmed through other people, through responding to their sometimes tactless and ill-directed comments. Most of them don't know all that much about us, and those who do are wary of Anton, and half afraid of me, because I possess what is known as a "vicious tongue" and make short work of petty fears and prejudices.

❧

Anton's affair with Anna Capriano continued but was from my point of view an outrage. By that time I was head over heels in love with him, admiring the way he sailed through his examinations, the way he looked and the way he was somehow inexplicably different. I worked sporadically with fringe theatre groups, independent troupes who hoped to explode many of the more cherished theatrical orthodoxies with a brave new vision. Critics no longer daunted me, for what could they know about acting unless they had experienced the living moment on a stage as we actors did. Besides, there was enormous safety in the jocosity of our numbers. My main preoccupation was to get a decent part in something as we moved from season to season, and generally speaking I managed. Anton saw me play Salomé, the best part I had ever had, and there's no doubt now that it changed everything. I was fitter than ever in my life before, conscious of the effect my dance before King

Herod had on the audience. I knew what it meant to be in the right place at the right time, to feel the power of life flowing in my veins. Anton told me afterwards that it woke him from his sleepy relationship with Anna and pulled him out of himself as nothing had done before.

Our wedding ceremony was short and unceremonious, our families and close friends filling the front pews of the cathedral in our home town. Beth read a poem, chosen by Anton. It was Vaughan's "Peace", which perplexed me considerably with its references to "a Countrie far beyond the stars" and the "beauteous files", presumably of the blessed. Yet I was happier than at any time in my life, although I would be sadder again before long.

"Oh Anton, Anton!" she cried on his shoulder in the church doorway afterwards. "Do be careful whatever you do..." She wept openly and with a sadness which left me perplexed, her mascara running in muddy little rivulets on either side of her nose.

"Look after him now!" she whispered fiercely, catching my wrist, matronly in a blue Jaeger dress and a matching hat with netting which quivered on her forehead.

"Of course I will," I assured her calmly, noting mentally that that was the third time I'd been asked to look after Anton in the general melee, with rice and confetti settling around us in the October air. It was what they called an Indian summer, the days full of translucence, every saw-toothed leaf tawny and fragile. On our way to the country house where the reception was held, we passed the old graveyard. The church was unchanged, but there was a grid across every window which would have made it impossible to force an entry. Anton looked at me.

"Do you remember?"

I nodded. We stayed late that day, remaining with our twenty guests who seemed in no great hurry to leave, then watched fireworks and the glow of distant bonfires on the horizon. There was nothing for Anton and me to hurry for, at least; the physical side of our relationship had long been established so the urgency of new passion was slightly muted. Still, by midnight he was pressing my arm, the pupils of his eyes large and shining. We slipped away to our room and left the others to their memories and the maudlin conversations which set in at the closing stages of weddings.

Part of my attraction to Anton has always been governed by a dull recognition that there was something about him which defied revelation. Over the next two years, although we were occupied and in most respects content, I felt something amiss. Looking back now I believe that some part of me knew but, uneasy about possible implications, had refused to acknowledge the truth. There had been signs, simple things, all along. I worked as irregularly as ever, occasionally striking lucky for a few months, but otherwise just looking on. I was particularly unhappy about not having been chosen for the part of Dora in a new play by Prendergast which was to tour America for six weeks. Resigned to tricking about with unchallenging roles, I returned home earlier than expected one Saturday morning after reading for a cameo which didn't in the least interest me.

"I'm ho-ome!" I called upstairs. Anton's work is

tiring, he often rests late on a Saturday. I heard rustling sounds. Thinking he was teasing me by remaining silent I took the stairs in twos, turned the landing and was stopped in my tracks.

He emerged from the bathroom. Clearly he hadn't heard me. He wore my silken robe. It fell open to reveal a satiny-looking bra, suspenders and lacy pants, dark glossy stockings covering his legs. His face was fully made-up, the eyes enhanced and made huge by eye-shadow and mascara.

"Let me explain..." he almost pleaded, as shocked as I was.

I stood there, slack-jawed, unable to utter a sound. Attempting to pull myself together I began to laugh nervously, to treat it as a joke.

"That's good, really good—is it your evening attire?"

I bent double, desperately hoping he'd agree, say it was all a joke, even if in bad taste. He stood watching me, then turned and walked into our bedroom, mincing effeminately in patent high heels which I registered as not being mine. I followed him, desperate for an explanation.

My breathing came in short little gasps as I went up to him and punched him in the chest, full on one of his ridiculous stuffed satin breasts.

"What the hell are you at?"

The words squeezed from my throat. I recognised symptoms of stage fright in myself. He said nothing. I struck him again, this time more forcefully.

"Tell me!" I whispered, my face wet with tears as I observed the man of my dreams who had been the boy of my dreams, whom I had always, always adored as if he were a pagan god, because he was so exceptional and so very lovely. People don't often describe men as "lovely" or "beautiful", but he was all that and more—elegant, erect, fully male.

"I've always been this way," he said, sitting on the bed as if exhausted.

"Why didn't you tell me?"

"I tried, couldn't get it out."

"Does anybody else know?"

The question was prompted not by fear of what people thought so much as a possessive need to be the first, the first to the experience which I found so utterly repulsive.

"Yes."

I began to feel faint. Someone else knew him better than I.

"Who?" I whispered, then more angrily "Who, for Christ's sake?"

I knew the answer without his telling, then felt all the angrier, all the more astounded.

"You can't be serious," I stuttered, rage rising like a white heat in my chest. He nodded slowly. Beth. Dear, innocent, helpless Beth, who understood nothing and was supposedly shockable, an impression she herself did little to allay. I would have preferred if it had been an affair, could have coped somehow with another woman, could deal with a sexual competitor. But this was beyond me. I hated them both for the collusion, Beth in particular for letting me patronise her, for never asserting that part of her personality which was ingenious, interesting, which I might have liked had she let me. Women are so detestably intelligent that the brightest subvert their talent into cunning and silence, as if they possessed no other means of power. That was Beth. Clued-in right from the start, tolerating, indulging my uninhibited nature, allowing me to think myself more perceptive than her, all along hugging her secret, avenging herself in silence.

"That traitor!" I muttered, slumping on to the bed beside him. "Your rotten, saccharine-sweet sneak of a sister could at least have told me, the poxy bitch."

He sat there, absurd, his face plastered inexpertly with my make-up. I tore around the room then, my limbs frozen yet violent, plundering drawers, wardrobe, turning automatically to his beside cabinet.

"There's nothing in here," he said, almost calmly. "Try the other room."

He took a packet of cigarettes from the pocket of my robe and lit one. I burst across the landing and into the spare bedroom. Still, I found nothing.

"Try the recess," he said helpfully.

The recess was where we kept wine, Christmas decorations, and boxes of useless items bought in second-hand shops, things like old photograph albums which we liked to rescue so that they'd have a home. The bottles broke on the carpet as I tossed them free of the two racks on which they rested, the air tangy with the scent of fermentation. I didn't care. Carpets, furniture, nothing mattered. Then I found it, a medium-sized box. It contained everything: basques, suspender-belts, bras, garters, slips, shimmering sets of knickers, silky stockings, the sort of article I never bought for myself but for which I'd always hankered. Things I'd have liked him to buy me, at Christmas or for birthdays or for no reason at all.

"You louse," I said simply, rising and turning towards where he stood in his pinks and creams, the silk robe still open.

"And for God's sake close that thing!" I snapped, leaving the room to pour myself a whiskey, cheated without fully understanding why. Hours later I could hear him upstairs, scrubbing the wine stains from the carpet. I pitied him then.

The funny thing was, we didn't sleep apart that night. I thought I'd want to, that he'd want to.

"I suppose I'd better move into the other room," he said.

It didn't work out like that at all. We were still friends. In the middle of the night we found ourselves embracing, and there was relief in that long embrace. Afterwards, I stroked his face, half-healed, but not fully. It was a moonlit night. I could see the outline of his brow and cheekbones.

"When did it begin?"

"You'll be surprised if I tell you," he said, turning on one side, his back to me, leaning in on my stomach.

"Tell me anyway."

"Around the time we broke into that church years back. You were prancing up and down on that altar like a demented sprite..."

I had looked wonderful, he told me, intriguing, feminine but wild, my skirt lifted to my waist.

"So?" I was flattered to think that he'd noticed me, that I'd been in any way striking at that stage in my gosling development.

"You whirled about and I saw your underwear." He listed the garments. A slip, the loose bloomers my mother had made me wear. Jesus, I thought.

"It was the first time I'd noticed women's things, how...soft and colourful they were... it's not sexual, not the way you imagine anyway..." he faltered.

"Would it have made a difference if I'd told you?" he asked then.

I turned away from him. Angry with myself as much as anything. Cheated. I needed to think. He went on and on about the freedom women have.

"I don't know." I answered sulkily.

꿩

Today he dresses more tastefully now that I've taken him in hand, though the underwear is still a big consideration. But I buy more interesting stuff for myself, which he approves of, and sensuousness can be expensive. The only thing I refuse is to accompany him down Grafton Street on a Saturday morning, when he's rigged out fully. I can't bear the possibility of running into someone who knows us, of observing them peer with curiosity at his jawline. The street is thronged with the young and fashionable, with pickpockets and photographers, with fortune-tellers, flower-sellers, people who trade on private dreams. Who knows what could happen. The best I can offer is an opinion on which skirt or dress is more suitable, which shoes are definitely out, which stockings enhance his legs. Once a week the house reeks of depilatory cream. He refuses to avail of the clean swipe of a razor, as I do, on the grounds that it makes the hair coarse. So he tells me.

Once a year we holiday abroad. On certain days we stroll as friends through the streets of ancient ports along the Mediterranean. On others we drift as lovers.

Either way, there are churches to be visited as a matter of course, where we sit and thrill to the sound of organ-music, to *bel canto*, to cantatas or a cor anglais vaulting into the baroque spaces above our heads. There is *fresco secco* showing scenes of unadulterated joy in which everyone is either robed flowingly, or naked. Then the splendid altars, exotic gargoyles, chorales of angels designed centuries ago by extravagant Italian sculptors. Finally an ancient dance remembered, part of us stirring, strong pagans within the resined infinities.

After The Match

They burst into the reception hall at Old Woodleigh, fists raised in triumph, the growing *waaahh* sound which had been audible from a distance now deepening, distorting their faces as they fell *en masse* through the double doors. The opposition had been trounced in a stunning display of muscle and airborne muck at the Leinster Schools Rugby Final.

Helen stood with Doreen and Katy, the wives of two other Bellemont teachers. *Waaahhh...* The women shifted uncomfortably, taking pointedly casual sips from their drinks as they watched the boys close in around the two trainers. Helen studied Adam's face. He was in seventh heaven. This was the moment when all the extra time spent training the young beasts—the late nights, the pep-talks and sessions which had intensified during the last, vital weeks—suddenly added up. She was pleased for him, the happy glow on his face some sort of pay off.

"Isn't it marvellous for them!" Doreen giggled over her G and T, adjusting a frothy pink blouse at the neck as the tangle of cheering bodies suddenly shifted in their direction.

"Absolutely!" Katy agreed. "You must both be

thrilled skinny."

"Oh it's great to see them win. As a mother I know just what it means to the boys," Doreen said, eyes shining with pleasure.

"Aren't you thrilled, Helen?" said Katy again, more for something to say than in true speculation.

"Delighted. Delighted," said Helen, distracted by the whooping and back-slapping.

"Of course it's your first time so it'll seem very new," said Doreen, conspiratorially. "But when Adam has worked with Patrick and brought them through like this a few more times, you'll take it all in your stride. I know when Patrick started training I was so nervous you wouldn't believe it. I mean you want them to win, you wish so desperately for everything to work out."

"Well it has anyway." Helen was vague, uncertain of her humour.

Patrick and Adam were hoisted shoulder-high, good-humouredly tolerating the heaving and jostling. The parents of the players mingled with the group, not quite at the centre of the knot of bodies but near enough to be hugged and kissed by sons who were out of their minds with joy. One of the boys forced the cup, a well-dented trophy chased in silver and gold, into Adam's hands.

"Ah, lads, I can't balance!" he shouted, raising the cup unsteadily. They roared again and took off at a lumbering gallop around the hall.

"Easy now lads!" Patrick called. Nobody heard. He was older than Adam, his face finely-lined, more assured.

Flustered helpers tried to seat the jubilant mob.

Waiters and serving women signalled, ignored until a few of the parents and most of the teachers made their way to the dining area. The boys followed untidily. Helen groaned quietly as one of them started the school rallying song again. It was rapidly taken up as they filtered through. She was starving. The afternoon on the terraces at Lansdowne had been freezing, hail and wind whipping in under the stand till they were drenched. They were proper ninnies to have taken so much trouble with their appearances, she thought, observing the other women. Like fresh, dewy flowers, individually not so interesting, but as a group colourful and strangely expectant. Like girls at their first party. The older ones were muffled in furs and fine wool. Because it was a day which had promised victory, she'd had her hair plaited, and wore a new navy and green dress bought specially for the occasion. It had cost too much but she liked it and Adam would find the effect exotic and interesting among all the matrons.

"*Womba, womba, womba,*" the slow chant began. She tried to look benevolent and pleasant as she took her seat and watched the team and their followers crash their way down along the tables. "*Ing-gang-oolie-oolie-oolie-oolie,*" they growled, reminding her of visiting rugby teams from New Zealand whose ritual dance was intended to intimidate the opponents. One of the boys grabbed a seat opposite her and sat down, panting.

"Jaysus!" he gasped, blinking in her direction, but she realised that he wasn't looking at her so much as drifting in and out of some hallucinatory and highly-pleasured dream. "*Ing-gang-goo.*"

To her right a restless middle-aged man with lightly-tanned skin shifted continually in his seat.

"Hello, I'm Helen Kilroy." She introduced herself easily, decided she'd best make an effort and be sociable. The bane of her life. Being sociable. Making an effort for the sake of civility. He looked at her for a moment, surprised at her presence, not expecting to be addressed.

"Oh. How d'you do? McElligot. Jim," he mumbled, extending his hand.

"You've a son on the team, right?"

"Wrong. Nephew," he said curtly, looking over her shoulder and waving at somebody.

"Good man Delaney! Knew you'd do it, ya bloody hound!" he bellowed, taking a slug from a glass of wine. "*Chow-chow-chow*," the call went, its barking rhythm strengthening. Helen tried again. For Adam's sake she must make an effort to be amenable.

"Oh yes, I remember the boy—Ciaran McElligot is your nephew."

"Got it in one!" he said, before stopping suddenly. "But...but...my God, I've just realised who you are!" He sat back, absorbing her from head to toe as if she were a vision.

"I do apologise Mrs Kilroy...Helen, that what you said?... The way things are today, I don't know what's happening. Super isn't it, you must be so proud of Adam, delighted with yourself, what?"

"*Womba, womba, womba.*" She wondered how to counter the flood of hyperbole. How pleased did she have to be, how could she convey her pleasure, that yes, it was wonderful?

To her left, Doreen chattered to somebody's father.

She was cut out for it, Helen thought, remembering the chocolate eclairs and apple-tarts which Doreen had ferried to the team the evening before every match. "I really feel for them," she was saying, staring wide-eyed at the man. "It's so hard for them in a boarding-school. I find they really need something to remind them that we all care, that somebody really, really cares."

"Oh you're quite right, quite right," the man replied politely.

The poor bugger was bored stiff. Helen peered pointedly over Doreen's shoulder and into his eyes. He caught the look and in the flicker of an instant almost responded, stifling a smile. She looked away then. No joy there. *Homo domesticus* if ever she saw him. Common-or-garden species. Widespread in the British Isles. Sheds its inhibitions only during summer migration. Likes the company of its own sex. Probably saves his charm for the rugby tours. Miles away from solicitous wives. Still. Best not start messing. For Adam's sake. Best behave and keep her talents for the home front or circles where they wouldn't be misinterpreted. This was no place for wit and irony. Or so much as a hint of sex. "*Yak-yak-yak-yak-yak-yak-yak,*" the boys roared. "*Come on, Bellemont, win it back!*" The "*Waaahh*" sound rose again as they finally settled down, plastic chairs scraping and hacking on the wooden floor.

Adam and Patrick sat like young bulls, penned off at the top table, surrounded by priests, the headmaster and various significant supports, including the priest who had once found her bathing naked with Adam in the school swimming-pool. Adam had been raging afterwards. Hadn't he told her not to strip, but no, she'd insisted, determined to tease, and had even tried to rip his swimming-trunks off, just as Goggle-face walked in. The thought of it made her suddenly splutter with laughter. The McElligot man peered at her closely.

"God but it's a tremendous occasion," he muttered to her, as if testing her sanity.

"God but it is," she replied glibly, giggling again in recollection of the priest's bland face as she'd waded to the side of the pool in an attempt to conceal her flesh. Word inevitably got around. A black mark. A man who couldn't control his wife in certain situations was open to question.

During the meal, people were absorbed in the post-mortem: the earnest dissection of every moment of play, comparisons with previous finals leading to disputes, jokes, noisy debate. She could think of a million and one more interesting topics, even if it was their special rugger day. Hadn't she shown interest in other people, even in the brat sitting opposite, hadn't she tried a variety of conversational options, from current affairs to UEFA and British soccer hooligans, the Olympics? Of course it wasn't necessary to say anything to that lot. She glared balefully at her soup. More a matter of making the right sounds, little-woman chat. She listened to Doreen.

"Well of course education is important, it's one of the most important things any parent can give a child!" she was saying with vehemence.

"Quite. The wife and I like to take certain decisions too. All in all some guidance is needed and the discipline which rugger adds is damn well unbeatable," the man beside her said.

"Discipline?" she cut in over Doreen's shoulder. "What do you mean by discipline?" she asked, putting on an interested face, hand curling under her chin. The man looked extremely surprised.

"Aaaah! Discipline? Discipline's discipline any way you look at it: the boys have to be ready to forge good careers, stand up for themselves, go for it in a tough world, that type of thing..."

A waiter slid a plate of turkey and ham before her, then another slammed a heap of mashed potatoes and liquidised sprouts on top of the meat.

"You mean externalised discipline?" Helen asked, determined to be awkward.

"What? Beg pardon?"

"The ability to kow-tow to authority and suchlike— a bit like doing things without asking why?"

Doreen nodded her head in agreement and Helen was suddenly aware that she was listening intently.

"But what else is there?" Doreen asked.

The man started to hum and haw.

"Asking why isn't always such a bally great thing, young woman," he commented, focusing thoughtfully at a point beyond her.

"You'd drive yourself crazy if you were constantly questioning things, Helen," said Doreen.

"Is that so?" said Helen.

"Yes, and the long and the short of it for me is that they get such a lot out of the experience. It stands to them, makes..." she searched for the word, "...it makes men of those boys."

"Well said, well said." The man applauded quietly with manicured hands.

The meal was over. There was, she thought, little to say which would have made the slightest difference. She glanced along the length of the table, making no effort to conceal an expression of boredom. Katy was chirruping with some guy from the IRFU, Doreen was flirting with the disciplinarian, McElligot brayed joyfully over his wine, his nephew smiled like an imbecile and the muscular boy opposite, who told her he was a hooker and laughed, expecting her not to understand what the term meant, rocked backwards and forwards on his chair, spooning trifle into his flaccid mouth. Adam and Patrick sat in the sanctuary of the top table. Thank God Adam wasn't a yob, one of those aleckadoos. At least the whole thing was a game for him, a sport. Rugby was rugby was rugby and if people didn't know the difference between Phase One and Phase Two possession they could forget it. Nor for him the ribald tribalism that emanated from their opponents' dressing-rooms prior to every match as trainers bullied mercilessly and told the team they couldn't generate a pint of piss between them. That wasn't Adam's style. Instead, Patrick had been persuaded to adopt Adam's half-baked meditation techniques, picked up as a result of some cursory reading and a trip to Bangkok some years back. The Bellemont boys had been ribbed mercilessly, with "Bellemont Boys Levitate" and "A Try for the Maharishi" lashed across the evening papers. All the more satisfying to prove them wrong, Helen thought, to see Adam have his glory. She was nothing if not loyal.

McElligot wheeled back in his chair as the speeches began. He had reached the point of no return, and lit a cigar unsteadily. The place was noisy: boys and fathers shouted and catcalled across the room; wives and mothers smiled in complicity, the *waaaahhh* sound threatening to erupt again until the headmaster raised his right arm in a plea for silence.

"Sieg heil!" somebody shouted from the back of the room. The whole place exploded.

"Dear colleagues," he finally began, "reverend fathers, parents, staff and—of course—students."

They yahooed long and loud. Tables were hammered, floors pounded with heavy feet.

There were at least five separate toasts and a few broken glasses. Helen's hands were sore from clapping. Nobody cared. This was Happyland. She knocked back her fifth glass of wine, face slightly numb, wanted to crawl into bed. Any long, wide, spacious area would do, somewhere she could wiggle her toes and open her bra. She helped herself to another drink. The red was good, fair dues to the priests. The headmaster was blathering on about history and the future, the importance of the Bellemont tradition and the splendid good fortune they'd had in their trainers.

"Hear, hear!" she called in a full, confident voice.

Doreen looked at her quizzically, then tittered.

"It's all right—I'm not pissed, just pissed off!" she whispered loudly. She waved at Adam. His attention was held by McElligot's nephew who was at that point unbuttoning his shirt. She tutted with impatience, as it came to her that her husband was as remote as he had ever been, perhaps as he had always been.

"But there are two people we especially want to

mention, to whom gratitude is due for their unstinting support, without whom much of what we achieved today might not have been possible."

He beamed down at them, his face radiating good intentions and assurance. There was a slight hush.

"Would Mrs Patrick Watson and Mrs Adam Kilroy care to stand and make themselves known?" he said good-humouredly.

Doreen stood up hesitantly, beckoning to Helen. "It's us, stand up!" she hissed uneasily. People applauded half-heartedly. Helen stayed sitting, her face pounding as two smirking boys waltzed down the length of the hall carrying bouquets. "*Waaahhh*" came the sound again as they were jeered on their way. The smoke from McElligot's cigar was cutting the back of her throat. Someone slapped her on the shoulders from behind and told her she must be proud as punch, as the flowers were plonked at her place.

"Well done, well done indeed, my dear," said McElligot.

"Congratulations! A wonderful day for Bellemont!" someone else called.

"Thank you," she said with what dignity she could summon.

Flowers. She simpered bitterly to herself. "*Ing-gang-oolie-oolie-oolie...*" Flowers for those who selflessly support the great endeavour. For rugger-hugging ladies. Healthy activity ze old rugby, she muttered to herself. The city hotels were flooded with women on the rampage during internationals, desperate because they'd reached thirty and might be left on the shelf, hungry for Frenchmen, Welshmen,

Scotsmen, any man who'd take them, willing to do or die for a life of leather balls and pungent socks. Good at the old rucking too, just like the lads in their own way, in for the kill. *"Womba, womba, womba."* Doreen looked pleased with herself, poked her face into the flowers time and again, saying wasn't it lovely of them, so thoughtful to think of such a thing, sure they'd done nothing to deserve it.

"When you make the sandwiches and cakes, that's what you get," Helen said loudly, then checked herself. Make an effort.

McElligot was reminiscing about his schooldays to nobody in particular.

"It's very nice of them all the same," Doreen insisted.

Helen was about to contradict her but stopped. What was the point when Doreen was so humble? Flowers. She didn't want anything. Being rewarded wasn't the point. The point—she took a deep breath— was that everybody pretended that the women were necessary to the scene, and the truth was they weren't. Which was fine with her but, by God, they needn't expect her to feel grateful.

"I wonder why everybody goes through the motions of thanking us?" she asked.

"Oh they're not just the motions, Helen!" said Doreen quickly. "It's well-meant, it's their way of saying something to us."

"Yeah, like fuck off, girls!"

Doreen raised her eyebrows, her jaw falling open.

"Sorry, sorry Doreen," said Helen. Oh Jesus, here we go again, apologising when there's fuck-all to be sorry for. The McElligot man cut in.

"They're saying thank you for putting up with this," he said in a wavering voice, his eyes moist and sentimental.

"Yip. It's a lot to put up with, isn't it?" said Helen.

"Ah now, ah now, it's not that bad."

"It's very important, Helen," said Doreen. "That's how the system works and it's very important for the boys.

"Of course it is, of course it is," Helen replied, folding her arms.

"There's no point resenting it, my dear," said McElligot with surprising lucidity.

"I don't resent it," she said lightly.

"But my dear lady, you've sat here all evening on sufferance. Mean to say, what are you, some sort of feminist or something?" he spat the question. She swallowed hard.

"Helen has her own ideas on everything," said Doreen in jolly tones, trying to smooth the atmosphere.

"I don't know how to answer you," said Helen. Her face was blotched, even her neck and chest felt hot. She caught a glimpse of Adam. Nabbed by yet another adoring mother ingratiating herself for a ray of his attention. Lapping it up. Both of them.

"Of course I'm a feminist," she responded, not knowing whether it was a lie or not. Weren't most of them ball-breakers anyway? McElligot raised his eyebrow in amusement.

"But I don't resent rugby. I just think it's given too much importance." She was hamming it up. Sounding resentful.

"In what way, my dear?" he asked, taking a puff from the cigar, his lips making a wet smacking sound as he inhaled. She could have shoved it down his throat.

"To enhance careers. Old boys network that kind of thing. It has damn all to do with sport."

"I see. But you're a feminist too—I don't meet too many of those—thought all that kind of thing had faded out in the early eighties really."

"No."

"Thought they were all lesbians too if you don't mind my saying so. You're not one of those, are you?" he chortled.

She laughed, because otherwise she might have wept.

"Ah well, I'll leave you to it, my dear. The wife's over there waiting; got to get home y'know. Nice meeting you, don't take it all so seriously."

He was gone, leaving a whiff of after-shave and cigar smoke in his wake. Reason and honesty didn't make for satisfaction when dealing with his sort. But neither did outrage. What he'd possibly expected. At her age she knew a few things. One of them was that most men would follow a ball or a pint across a roomful of naked sylphs, much like the joke said. The other was that women were always on the losing team, whichever way you looked at it. The trouble was, she couldn't figure out whether it was types like Doreen or types like herself who were the greatest fools. Doreen could sit back modestly, like an artless virgin, all self-effacement and wide eyes and got along grand. She, on the other hand, didn't even bother to conceal her feelings, or when she thought about it, to use her attractiveness. When she felt sour it showed. Men could sniff out womanish discontent and rebellion wherever it lurked. Doreen seemed spot on. For the umpteenth time she wondered why the hell it mattered what men thought about women. And then again maybe she'd been codding herself. Look at Doreen. A decent skin. A nice woman who worked hard at keeping Patrick happy, doing what she thought he wanted.

"*Womba, womba, womba.*" There it was again. The boys had formed a train and shuffled Maori-style around the two trainers. "*Ing-gang-oolie-oolie-oolie-oolie-oolie.*" Gathering her bag and jacket, the green one borrowed from her sister to match the dress, so that she'd look well on the day, she stared at Adam. He was like a god to the boys, even looked like one, a colossus, in command, the glow of victory on his smooth brow. Patrick was more avuncular, a sort of tribal chief. If this were the Amazon jungle, she thought, the rites of passage would be somewhat different. Circumcision with a piece of flint. A bit of vine-swinging. Ritual raping and pillaging instead of socialised aggression. A time for the elders to pass on the wisdom of their sex, the lore of centuries. They were getting their lore today, all right, messages in abundance. How to live. Entitlements. An inheritance.

She turned in disgruntlement to Doreen. "How did Patrick enjoy Paris?"

"Had a ball, won all their matches—didn't Adam tell you?"

"He did. Just wondering how Patrick found it."

Patrick had drunk himself footless one night, the gendarmes eventually prising him from a restaurant into which he'd staggered, wearing a balaclava, shouting something about *un petit hold-up.*

"It's all right Helen—I know what happened," said Doreen.

"What?"

"He rang me up in the middle of the night singing the Can-Can."

"Oh."

"Count yourself lucky that at least Adam's no boozer," she added. The tables were turned. But Helen didn't mind. It was common knowledge. She was used to it. Adam's French floozie. Adam's bonbon, sweetmeat or whatever. He'd told her himself, guilt-ridden, full of boyish remorse.

"Men," she said grimly.

"Bastards."

"Have you been drinking?" Helen asked, unaccustomed to Doreen's directness.

"Two G and T's. It's such a load of shit, isn't it?"

"Wish I'd never set foot in the place."

It was a kind of truce, an acknowledgement of some essential base-line failure on both sides.

"Would you look at them!" Doreen spat in outright mockery.

"Boys will be boys as they say!"

"*Chow-chow-chow.*" In this setting, she didn't recognise Adam. This was what he escaped to, like all men in flight from women. He looked innocently past her, certain of his life, its correctness. Through it all, she did not exist.

"Are you staying, or d'you want a lift?" she called to Doreen. Let him find his own way home.

"I'll come: God knows where the carry-on'll end tonight."

"*Yak-yak-yak-yak-yak-yak-yak.*"

"Your hair's gorgeous," she said companionably.

"Oh, look the flowers—"

"Leave them," said Helen irritably.

The crowd had dispersed slightly. The atmosphere was damp and beery, like a hotel after a hooley. Forlorn. She stood at the exit and searched for the car-keys. It was drizzling. Outside, daffodils wavered unsteadily. But the light was spring-like despite the needling cold. And the season was over. Her husband would gradually shed his inattention. He would be hers again in some limited way. He might want her, might learn that she was more than a sanctuary of peace. He might actually desire her. That was what mattered. It was why so many women turned out in force. Hanging on to men they loved in some quirky way. *"Yak-yak-yak-yak-yak-yak-yak,"* the sound faded as the two women hurried across the carpark. The main road was blocked with traffic.

"Will we go somewhere?" said Doreen, straightening her coat as she sat into the car.

"What? You mean not go home? Entertainment?"

"I wonder what Bad Bobs is like?"

"Full of men. Have you any money?"

"Cheque book," said Doreen, opening a bottle of perfume and spraying both wrists.

"That'll do. Let's go," said Helen, her expression set.

She fastened the seat-belt, listened for a moment to the distant *"waaahhh"* sound and revved up. She was ready for anything.

꙰꙰꙰

258